THE CASAGRANDES™

"FRIENDS AND FAMILY"

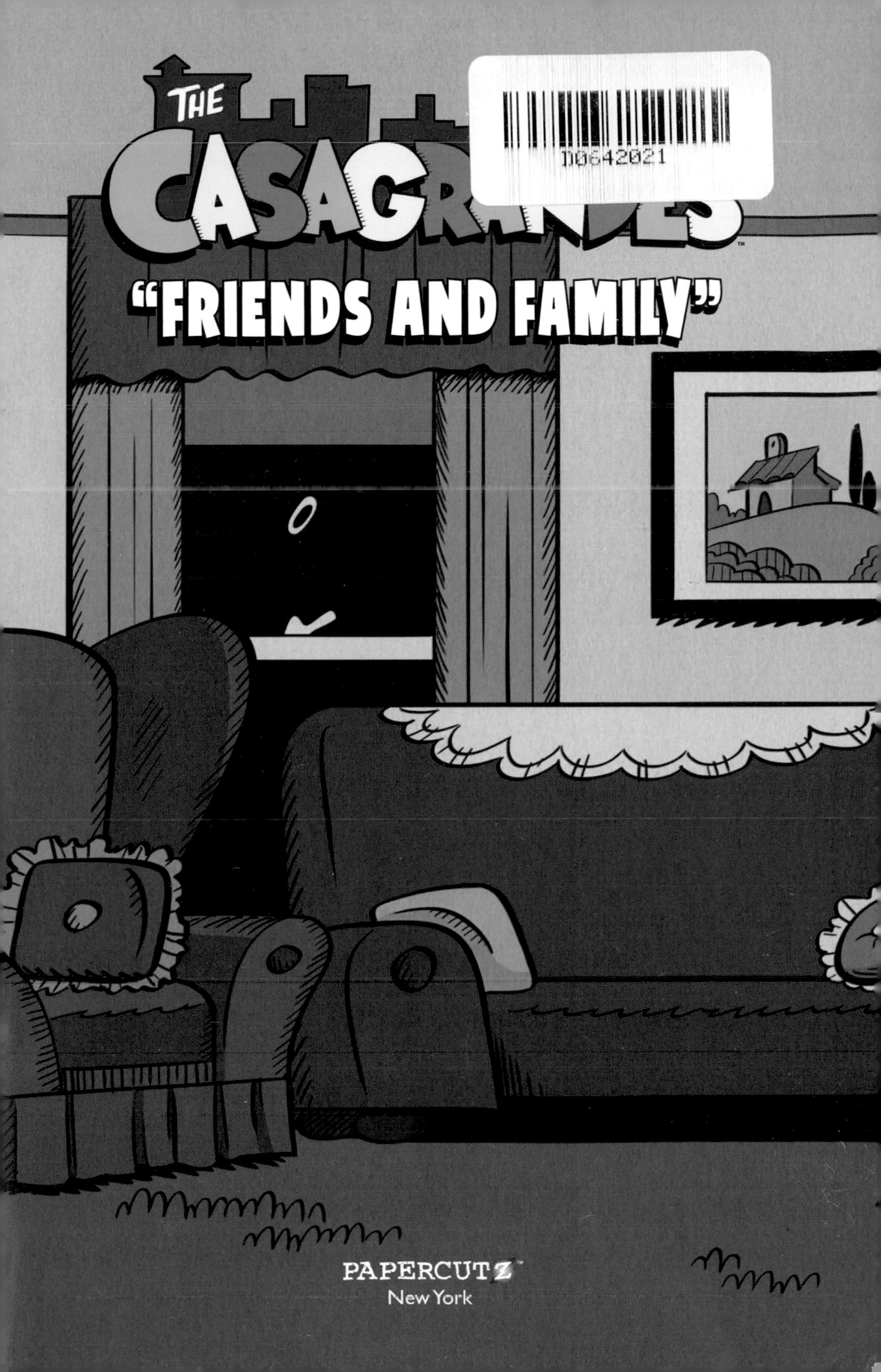

PAPERCUTZ™
New York

MORE GREAT GRAPHIC NOVEL SERIES AVAILABLE FROM

PAPERCUTZ™

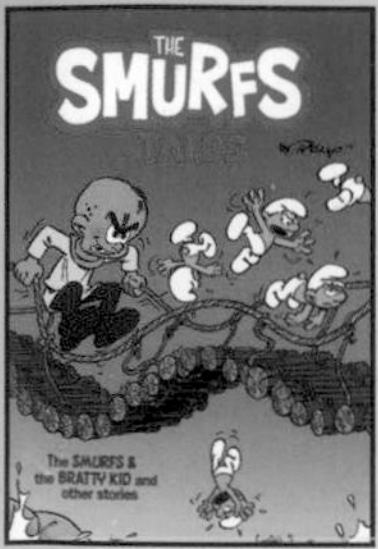
THE SMURFS
The SMURFS & the BRATTY KID and other stories

THE SMURFS TALES

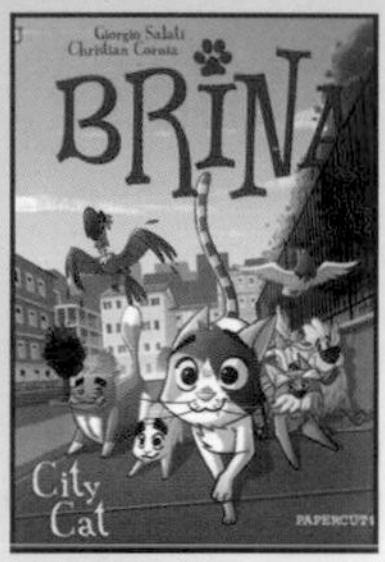
Giorgio Salati
Christian Cornia
BRINA
City Cat
PAPERCUTZ

BRINA THE CAT

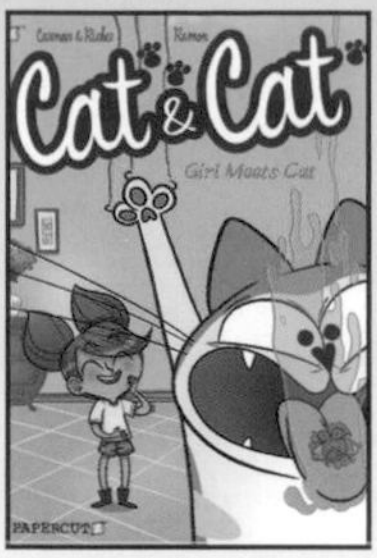
Cat & Cat
Girl Meets Cat
PAPERCUTZ

CAT & CAT

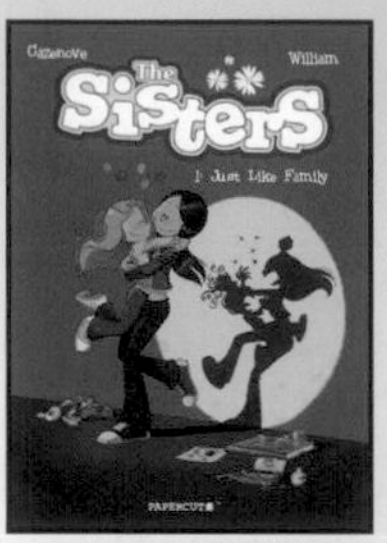
Cazenove
William
The Sisters
1: Just Like Family
PAPERCUTZ

THE SISTERS

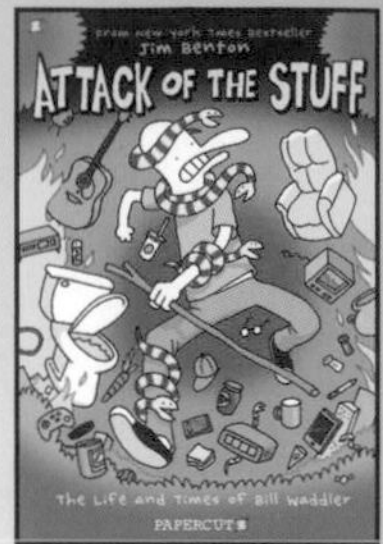
Jim Benton
ATTACK OF THE STUFF
The Life and Times of Bill Waddler
PAPERCUTZ

ATTACK OF THE STUFF

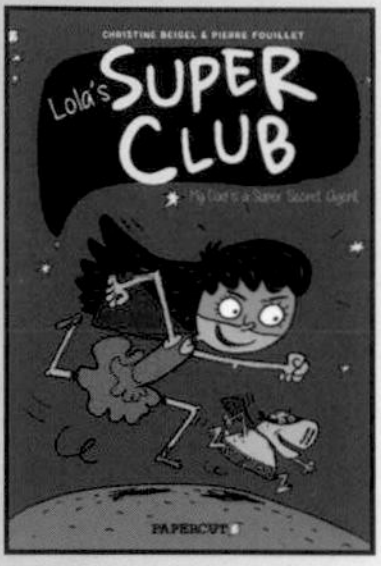
CHRISTINE BEIGEL & PIERRE FOUILLET
Lola's SUPER CLUB
PAPERCUTZ

LOLA'S SUPER CLUB

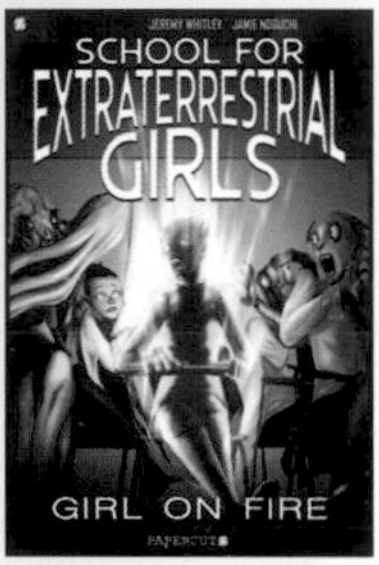
JEREMY WHITLEY
JAMIE NOGUCHI
SCHOOL FOR EXTRATERRESTRIAL GIRLS
GIRL ON FIRE
PAPERCUTZ

SCHOOL FOR EXTRATERRESTRIAL GIRLS

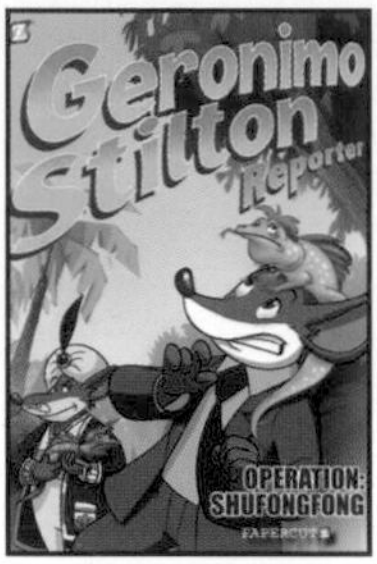
Geronimo Stilton
Reporter
OPERATION: SHUFONGFONG
PAPERCUTZ

GERONIMO STILTON REPORTER

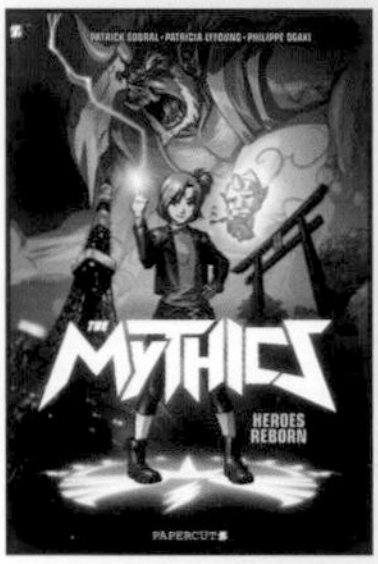
PATRICK SOBRAL · PATRICIA LYFOUNG · PHILIPPE OGAKI
THE MYTHICS
HEROES REBORN
PAPERCUTZ

THE MYTHICS

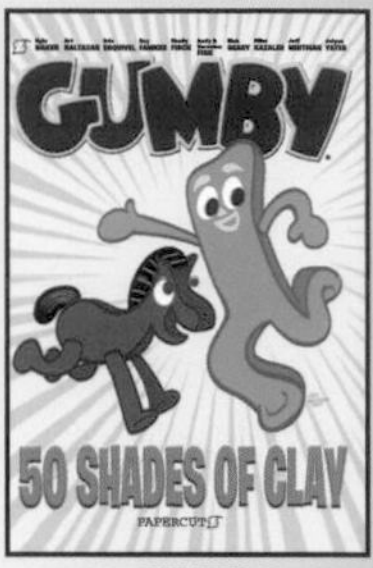
GUMBY
50 SHADES OF CLAY
PAPERCUTZ

GUMBY

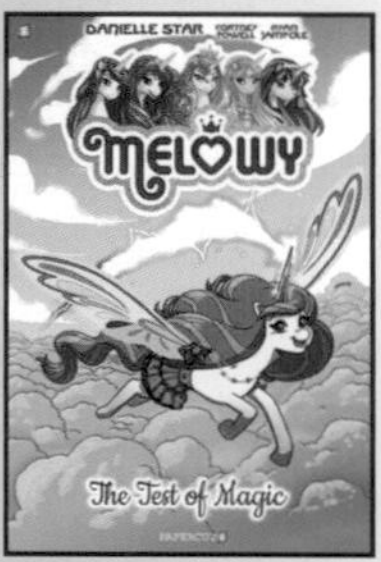
DANIELLE STAR
MELOWY
The Test of Magic
PAPERCUTZ

MELOWY

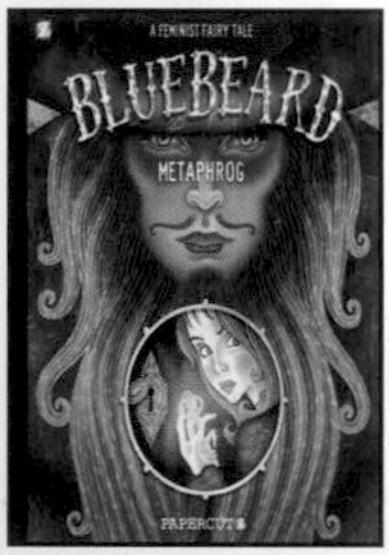
A FEMINIST FAIRY TALE
BLUEBEARD
METAPHROG
PAPERCUTZ

BLUEBEARD

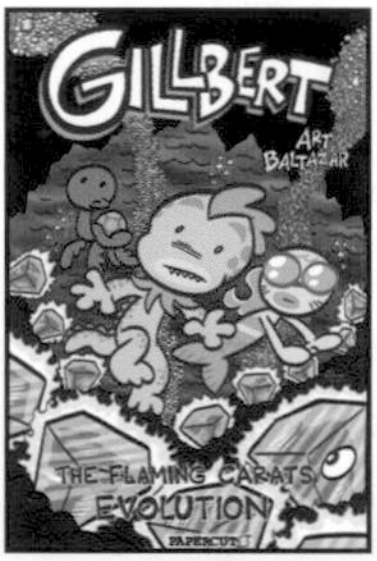
GILLBERT
ART BALTAZAR
THE FLAMING CARATS
EVOLUTION
PAPERCUTZ

GILLBERT

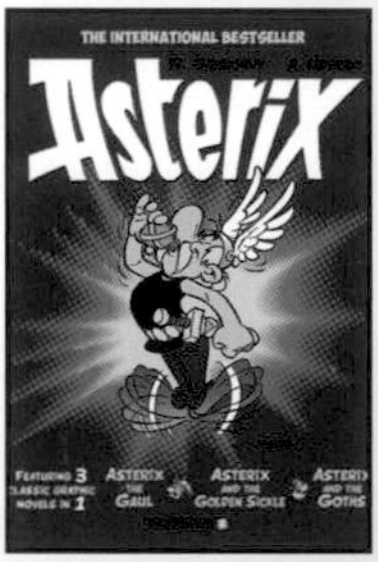
THE INTERNATIONAL BESTSELLER
Asterix
FEATURING 3 CLASSIC GRAPHIC NOVELS IN 1
ASTERIX THE GAUL
ASTERIX AND THE GOLDEN SICKLE
ASTERIX AND THE GOTHS

ASTERIX

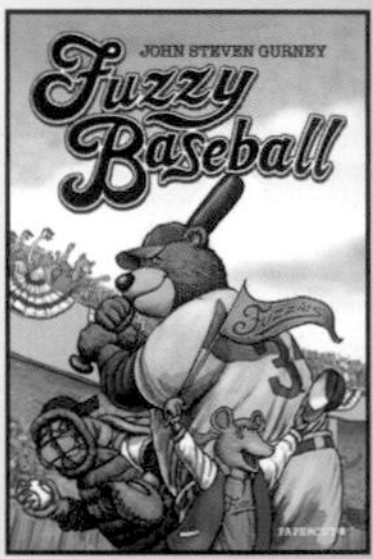
JOHN STEVEN GURNEY
Fuzzy Baseball

FUZZY BASEBALL

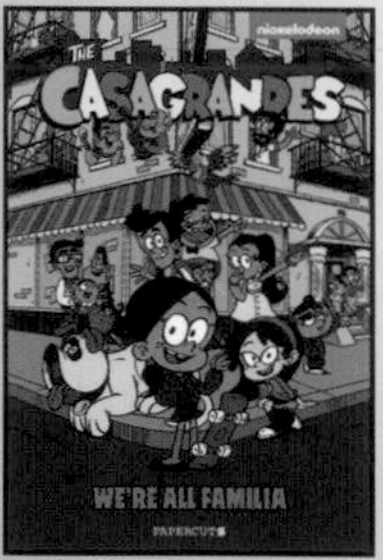
nickelodeon
THE CASAGRANDES
WE'RE ALL FAMILIA
PAPERCUTZ

THE CASAGRANDES

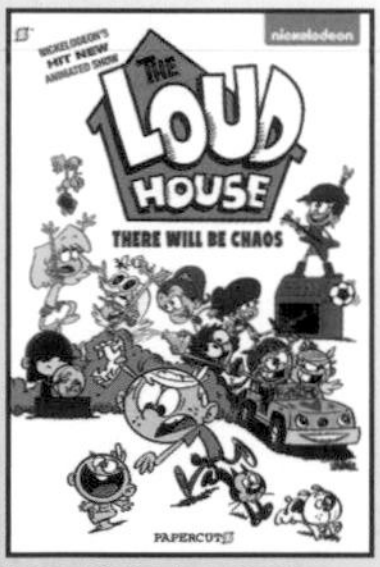
nickelodeon
THE LOUD HOUSE
THERE WILL BE CHAOS
PAPERCUTZ

THE LOUD HOUSE

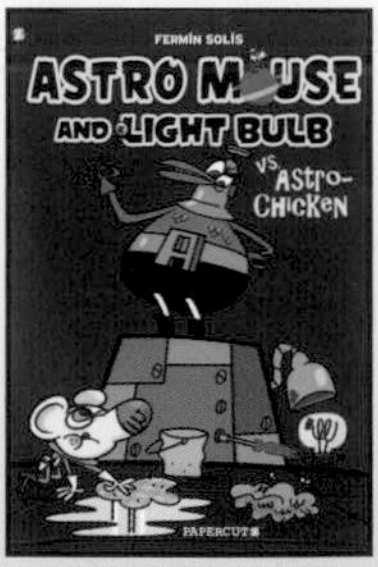
FERMÍN SOLÍS
ASTRO MOUSE AND LIGHT BULB
VS ASTRO-CHICKEN
PAPERCUTZ

ASTRO MOUSE AND LIGHT BULB

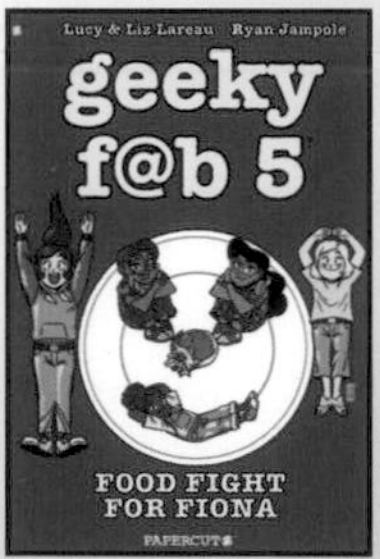
Lucy & Liz Lareau
Ryan Jampole
geeky f@b 5
FOOD FIGHT FOR FIONA
PAPERCUTZ

GEEKY F@B 5

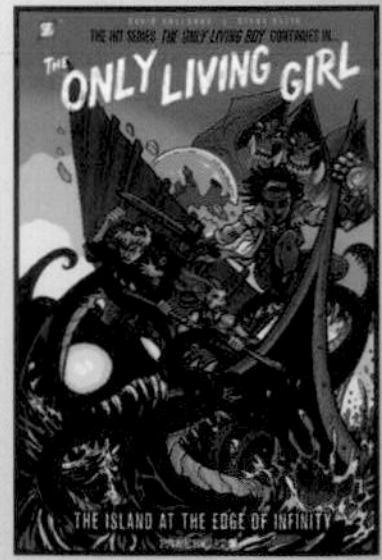
THE ONLY LIVING GIRL
THE ISLAND AT THE EDGE OF INFINITY
PAPERCUTZ

THE ONLY LIVING GIRL

papercutz.com

Also available where ebooks are sold.

THE CASAGRANDES

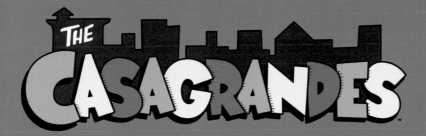

#4 "FRIENDS AND FAMILY"

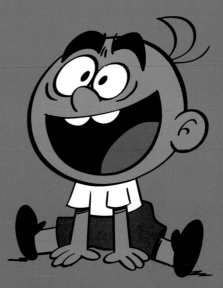

nickelodeon THE CASAGRANDES #4 "FRIENDS AND FAMILY"

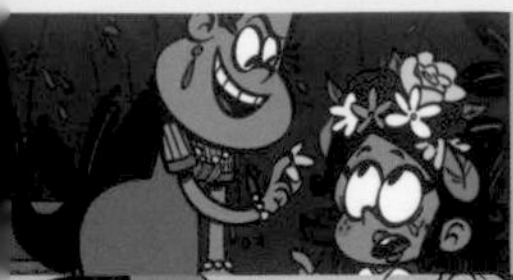

"GODDESS INSPIRED"
Kara Fein — Writer
Lex Hobson — Artist, Colorist
Wilson Ramos Jr. — Letterer

"SELL BY LATE"
Amanda Fein — Writer
Erin Hyde — Artist, Colorist
Wilson Ramos Jr. — Letterer

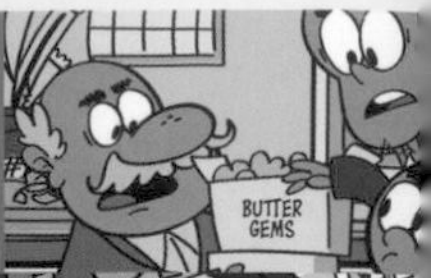
BUTTER GEMS

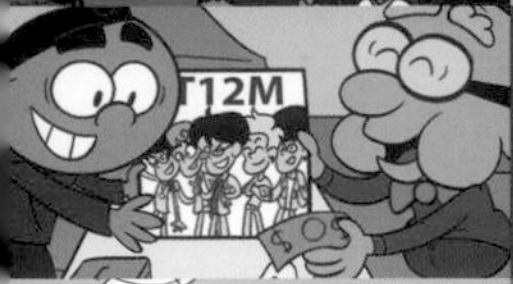
T12M

"BARGAIN HUNT"
Paloma Uribe — Writer
Izzy Boyce-Blanchard — Artist
Erin Rodriguez — Colorist
Wilson Ramos Jr. — Letterer

"THAT'S THE SPIRIT"
Derek Fridolfs — Writer
Zazo Aguiar — Artist, Colorist
Wilson Ramos Jr. — Letterer

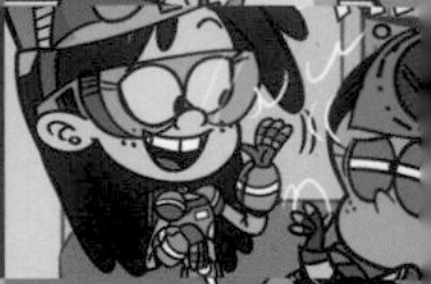

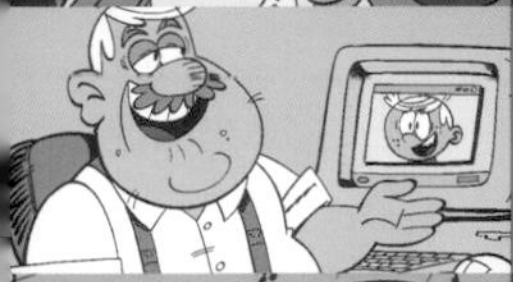

"POP UP"
Derek Fridolfs — Writer
Ryan Jampole — Artist
Laurie Smith — Colorist
Wilson Ramos Jr. — Letterer

"MEATBALL MANIA"
Kara Fein — Writer
Alexia Valentine — Artist
Lex Hobson — Colorist
Wilson Ramos Jr. — Letterer

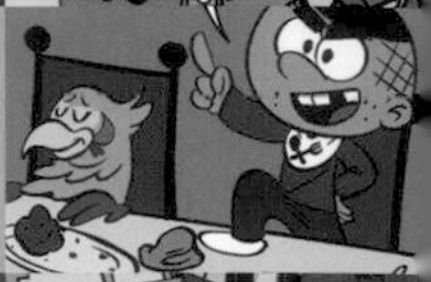

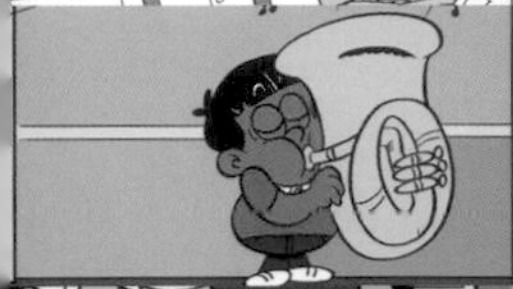

"TUBADOUR"
Derek Fridolfs — Writer
Alexia Valentine — Artist
Erin Rodriguez — Colorist
Wilson Ramos Jr. — Letterer

"ALL NIGHTER"
Caitlyn Connelly — Writer
Jose Hernandez — Artist
Erin Rodriguez — Colorist
Wilson Ramos Jr. — Letterer

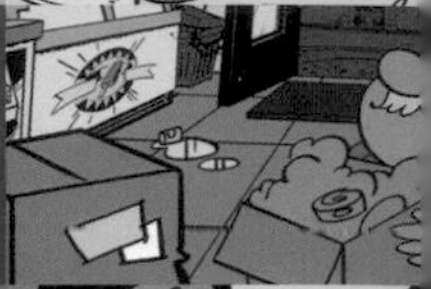

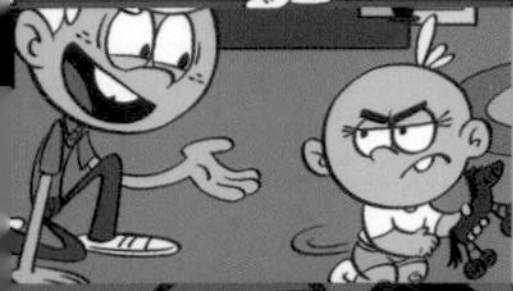

"HUNT FROM HOME"
Caitlyn Connelly — Writer
Alexia Valentine — Artist
Erin Rodriguez — Colorist
Wilson Ramos Jr. — Letterer

"BACK TO THE BOOGIE"
Caitlyn Connelly — Writer
Izzy Boyce-Blanchard — Artist, Colorist
Wilson Ramos Jr. — Letterer

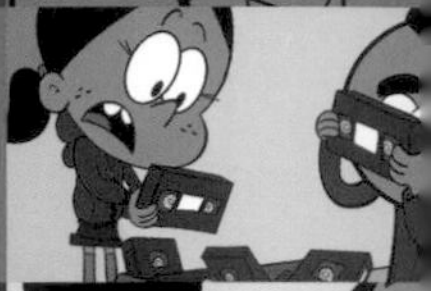

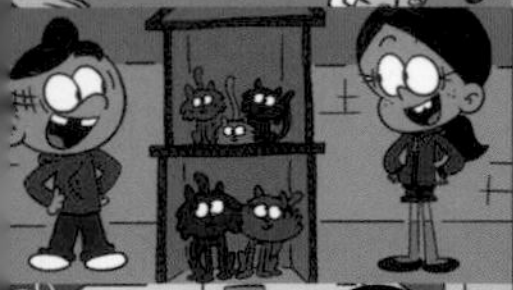

"MEOW OR NEVER"
Paloma Uribe — Writer
Amanda Tran — Artist, Colorist
Wilson Ramos Jr. — Letterer

"SPAR WITH PAR"
Kacey Huang Wooly — Writer
Erin Hyde — Artist, Colorist
Wilson Ramos Jr. — Letterer

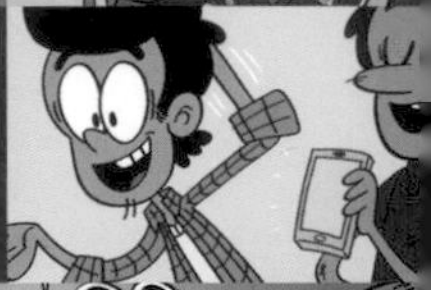

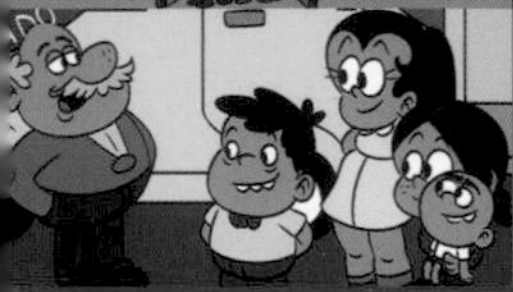

"THE MEET UP"
Derek Fridolfs — Writer
D.K. Terrell — Artist, Colorist
Wilson Ramos Jr. — Letterer

"TRENDFRETTER"
Erik Steinman — Writer
Lex Hobson — Artist, Colorist
Wilson Ramos Jr. — Letterer

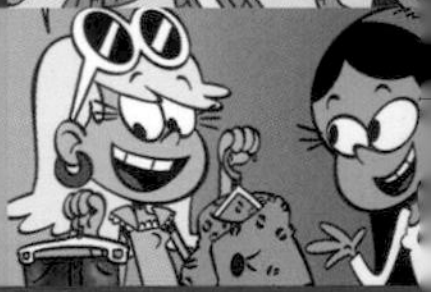

MIGUEL GONZALEZ — Cover Artist
JAYJAY JACKSON — Design
DANA CLUVERIUS, MOLLIE FREILICH, NEIL WADE, MIGUEL PUGA, LALO ALCARAZ, JOAN HILTY,
KRISTEN YU-UM, EMILIE CRUZ, and ARTHUR "DJ" DESIN — Special Thanks
KARLO ANTUNES — Editor
STEPHANIE BROOKS — Assistant Managing Editor
JEFF WHITMAN — Comics Editor/Nickelodeon
MICOL HIATT — Comics Designer/Nickelodeon
JIM SALICRUP
Editor-in-Chief

ISBN: 978-1-5458-0963-1 paperback edition
ISBN: 978-1-5458-0964-8 hardcover edition

www.papercutz.com

Papercutz books may be purchased for business or promotional use. For information on bulk purchases please contact Macmillan Corporate and Premium Sales Department at (800) 221-7945 x5442.

Printed in China
September 2022

Distributed by Macmillan
First Printing

THE CASAGRANDES

Theme Song Performed by: ALLY BROOKE
Theme Song Composed by: GERMAINE FRANCO
Lyrics by: GERMAINE FRANCO, MIKE RUBINER & LALO ALCARAZ
Rap Lyrics Performed by: IZABELLA ALVAREZ

I'm in the big city with my big familia [family]

Everyday here is my favorite día [day]

One big house and our family store
Food and laughter ¡y mucho amor! [and a lot of love!]

Tíos [aunts and uncles], abuelos [grandparents], all of my primos [cousins]...

A dog, a parrot, amigos! [friends!]

We're one big family now!
Sundays and Mondays
They're all fun days when you're with the...
Casagrandes!
¡Mucha vida! [A lot of life!]

Casagrandes!
¡Bienvenida! [Welcome!]

Casagrandes!
¡Mucha risa! [A lot of laughs!]

Casagrandes!
We're all familia! [Family!]

¡Tan-tan! [Tah-dah!]

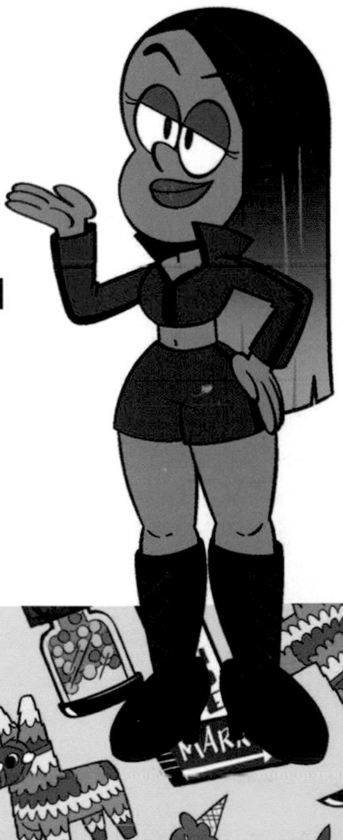

MEET THE CASAGRANDES *and friends!*

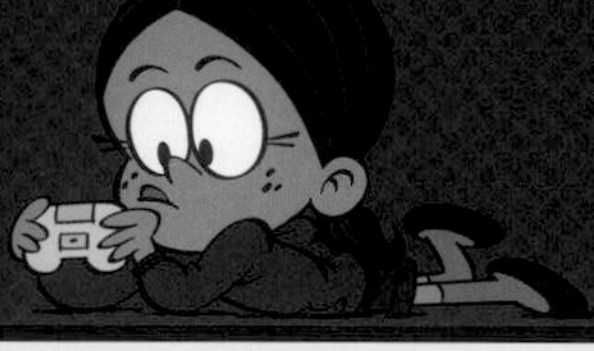

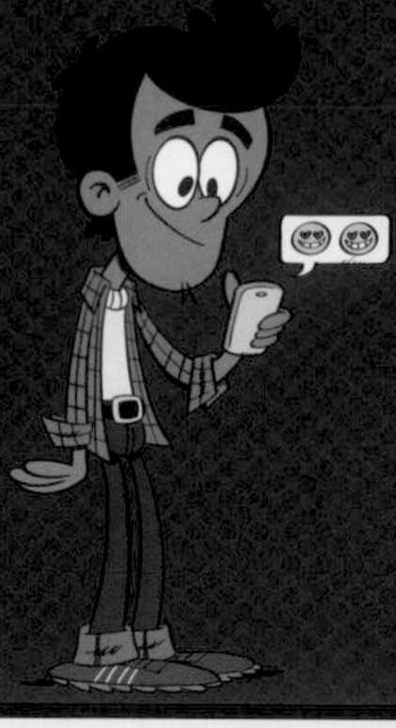

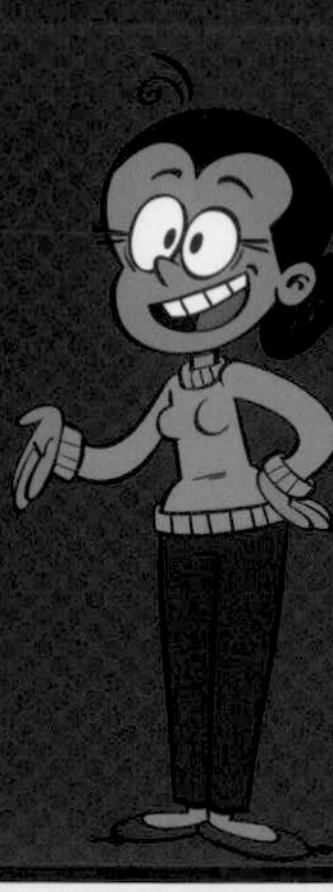

RONNIE ANNE SANTIAGO

Ronnie Anne's a skateboarding city girl now. She's fearless, free-spirited, and always quick to come up with a plan. She's one tough cookie, but she also has a sweet side. Ronnie Anne loves helping her family, and that's taught her to help others too. When she's not pitching in at the family *mercado*, you can find her exploring the neighborhood with her best friend Sid, or ordering hot dogs with her skater buds Casey, Nikki, and Sameer. Having a family as big as the Casagrandes has taught Ronnie Anne to deal with anything life throws her way.

BOBBY SANTIAGO

Bobby is Ronnie Anne's big bro. He's a student and one of the hardest workers in the city. He loves his family and loves working at the *mercado*. As his *abuelo's* right hand man, Bobby can't wait to take over the family business one day. He's a big kid at heart, and his clumsiness gets him into some sticky situations at work, like locking himself in the freezer. *Mercado* mishaps aside, everyone in the neighborhood loves to come to the store and talk to Bobby.

MARIA CASAGRANDE SANTIAGO

Maria is Bobby and Ronnie Anne's mom. As a nurse at the city hospital, she's hardworking and even harder to gross out. For years, Maria, Bobby, and Ronnie Anne were used to only having each other… but now that they've moved in with their Casagrande relatives, they're embracing big family life. Maria is the voice of reason in the household and known for her always-on-the-go attitude. Her long work hours means she doesn't always get to spend time with Bobby and Ronnie Anne; but when she does, she makes that time count.

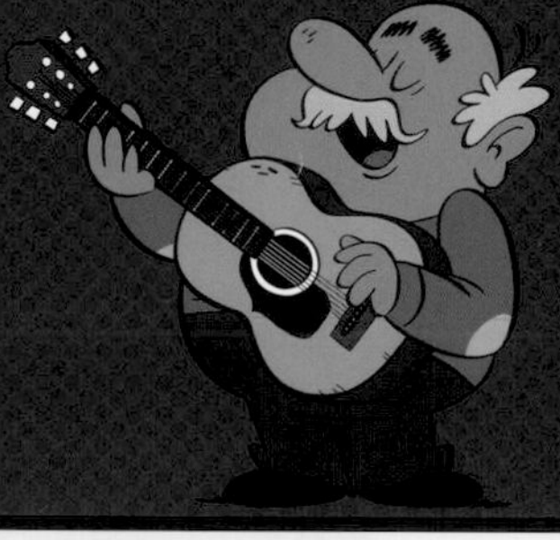

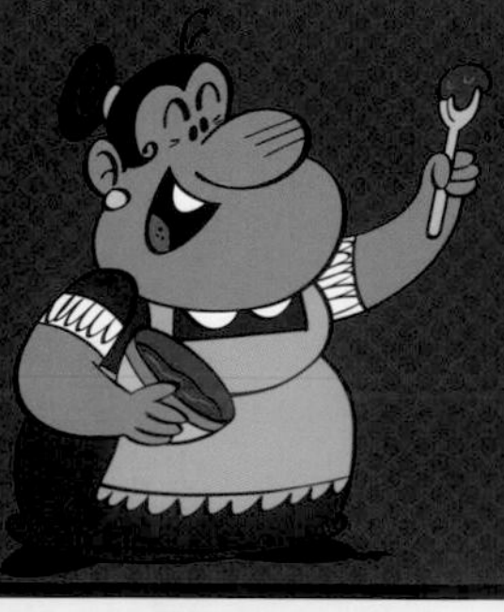

HECTOR CASAGRANDE

Hector is Carlos and Maria's dad, and the *abuelo* of the family (that means grandpa)! He owns the *mercado* on the ground floor of their apartment building and takes great pride in his work, his family, and being the unofficial "mayor" of the block. He loves to tell stories, share his ideas, and gossip (even though he won't admit to it). You can find him working in the *mercado*, playing guitar, or watching his favorite *telenovela*.

ROSA CASAGRANDE

Rosa is Carlos and Maria's mom and the *abuela* of the family (that means grandma)! She's the head of the household, the wisest Casagrande, and the master cook with a superhuman ability to tell when anyone in the house is hungry. She often tries to fix problems or illnesses with traditional Mexican home remedies and potions. She's very protective of her family… sometimes a little too much.

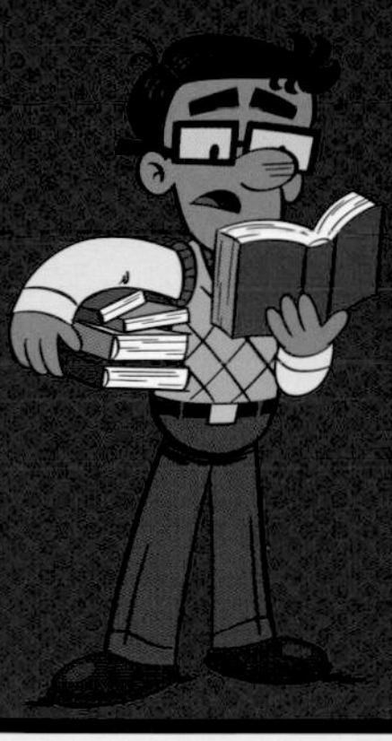

CARLOS CASAGRANDE

Carlos is Maria's brother. He's married to Frida, and together they have four kids: Carlota, C.J., Carl, and Carlitos. Carlos is a Professor of Cultural Studies at a local college. Usually he has his head in the clouds or his nose in a textbook. Relatively easygoing, Carlos is a loving father and an enthusiastic teacher who tries to get his kids interested in their Mexican heritage.

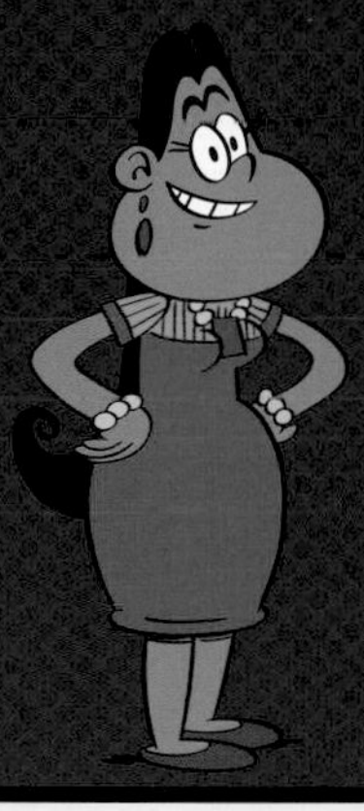

FRIDA PUGA CASAGRANDE

Frida is Carlota, C.J., Carl, and Carlitos' mom. She's an art professor and a performance artist, and is always looking for new ways to express herself. She's got a big heart and isn't shy about her emotions. Frida tends to cry when she's sad, happy, angry, or any other emotion you can think of. She's always up for fun, is passionate about her art, and loves her family more than anything.

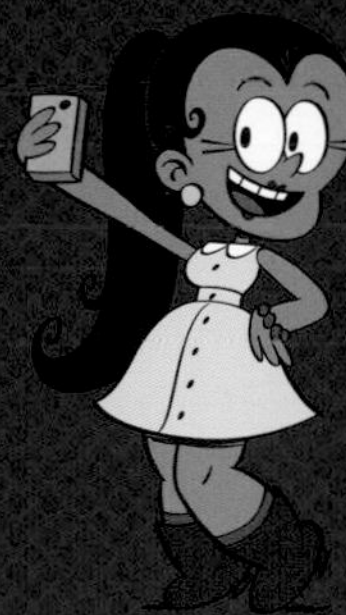

CARLOTA CASAGRANDE

Carlota is CJ, Carl, and Carlitos' older sister. A social media influencer, she's excited to be like a big sister to Ronnie Anne. She's a force to be reckoned with, and is always trying to share her distinctive vintage style tips with Ronnie Anne.

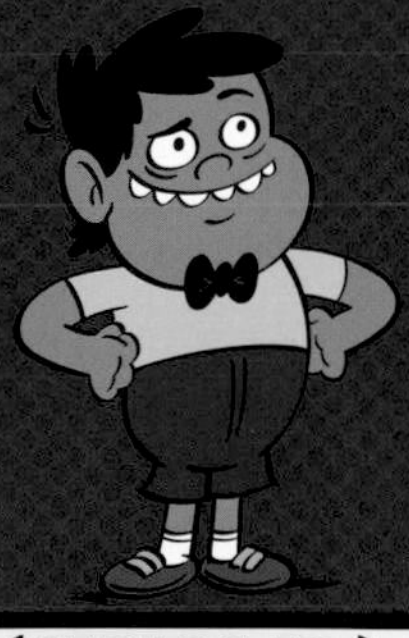

CJ (CARLOS JR.) CASAGRANDE

CJ is Carlota's younger brother and Carl and Carlitos' older brother. He was born with Down Syndrome. He lights up any room with his infectious smile and is always ready to play. He's obsessed with pirates and is BFFs with Bobby. He likes to wear a bowtie to any family occasion, and you can always catch him laughing or helping his *abuela*.

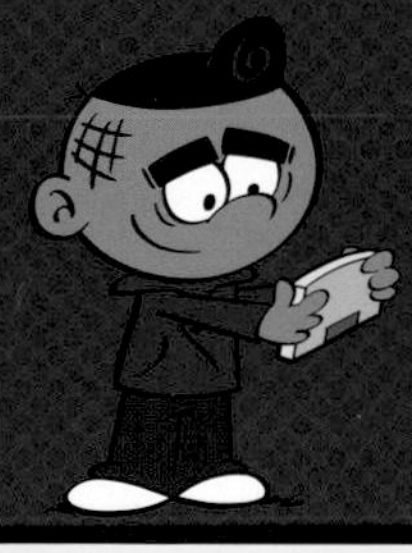

CARL CASAGRANDE

Carl is wise beyond his years. He's confident, outgoing, and puts a lot of time and effort into looking good. He likes to think of himself as a suave businessman and doesn't like to get caught playing with his action figures or wearing his footie PJs. Even though Bobby is nothing but nice to him, Carl sees his big cousin as his biggest rival.

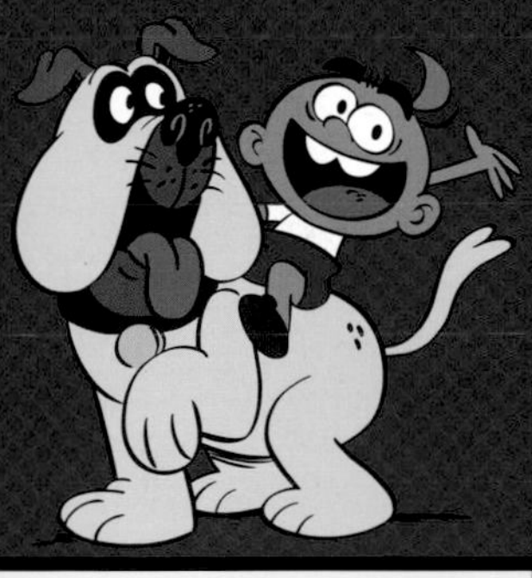

CARLITOS CASAGRANDE

Carlitos is the baby of the family, and is always copying the behavior of everyone in the household—even if they aren't human. He's a playful and silly baby who loves to play with the family pets.

LALO

Lalo is a slobbery bull mastiff who thinks he's a lapdog. He's not the smartest pup, and gets scared easily… but he loves his family and loves to cuddle.

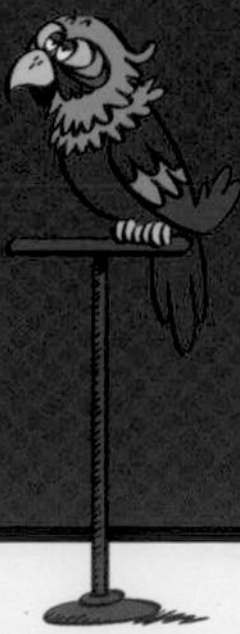

SERGIO

Sergio is the Casagrandes' beloved pet parrot. He's a blunt, sassy bird who "thinks" he's full of wisdom and always has something to say. The Casagrandes have to keep a close eye on their credit card as Sergio is addicted to online shopping and is always asking the family to buy him some new gadget he saw on TV. Sergio is most loyal to Rosa and serves as her wing-man, partner-in-crime, taste-tester, and confidant. Sergio is quite popular in the neighborhood and is always up for a good time. When he's not working part time at the *mercado* (aka messing with Bobby), he can be found hanging with his roommate Ronnie Anne, partying with Sancho and his other pigeon pals, or trying to get his ex-girlfriend, Priscilla (an ostrich at the zoo), to respond to him.

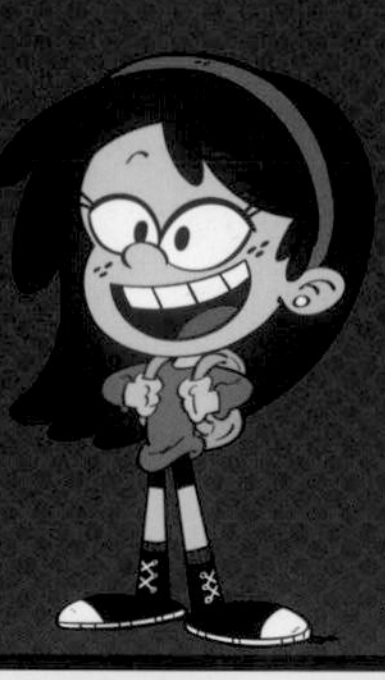

SID CHANG

Sid is Ronnie Anne's quirky best friend. She's new to the city but dives headfirst into everything she finds interesting. She and her family just moved into the apartment one floor above the Casagrandes. In fact, Sid's bedroom is right above Ronnie Anne's. A dream come true for any BFFs.

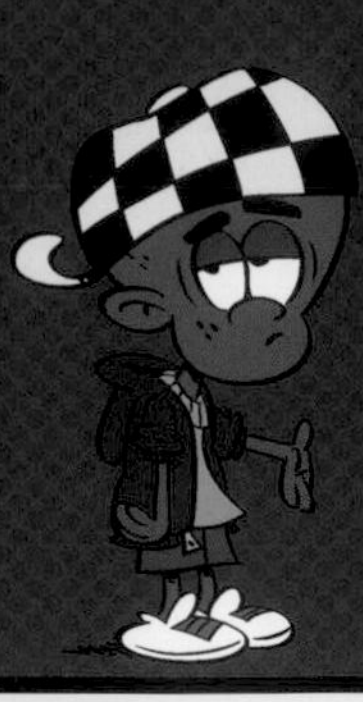

CASEY

Casey is a happy-go-lucky kid who's always there to help. He knows all the best spots to get grub in Great Lakes City. When he is not skateboarding with the crew, he loves working with his dad, Alberto, on their Cubano sandwich food truck.

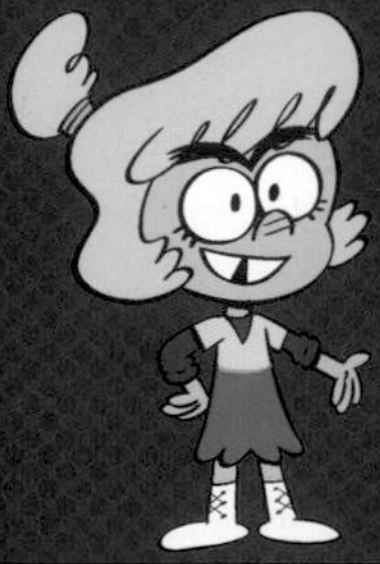

BECKY

A tough as nails classmate of Ronnie Anne and the skater kids. She makes a good match for her girlfriend, Dodge, captain of the Chavez Academy dodgeball team. Becky has a taste for chaos and destruction that she shares with her younger brother, Ricky, and her loyal dog, Malo. In a pinch though, Becky will definitely come through for a friend in need!

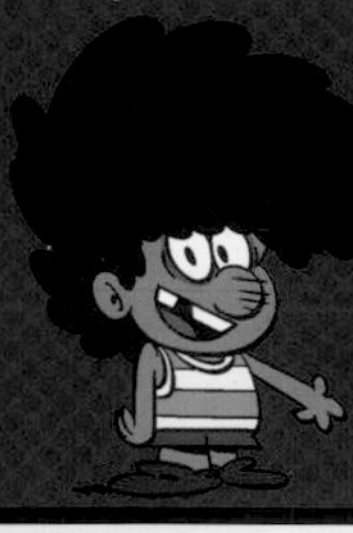

SAMEER

Sameer is a goofy sweetheart who wishes he was taller, but what he lacks in height, he makes up for with his impressive hair and sweet skate moves. He is always down for the unexpected adventure and loves entertaining his friends with his spooky tales!

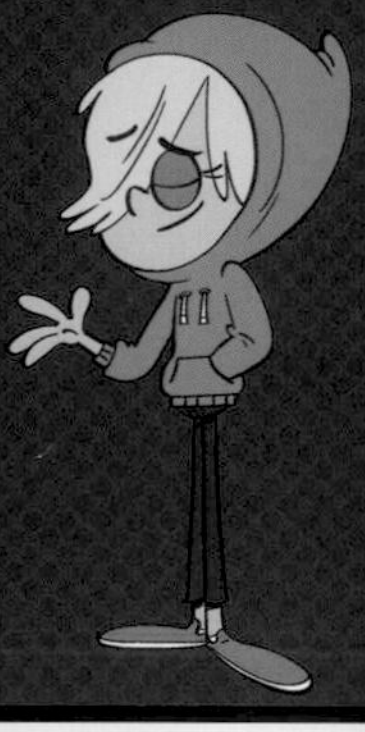

NIKKI

Nikki is as daring as she is easygoing and laughs when she is nervous. When she's not hanging with her buds at the skatepark, she likes checking out the newest sneakers and reading books about the paranormal.

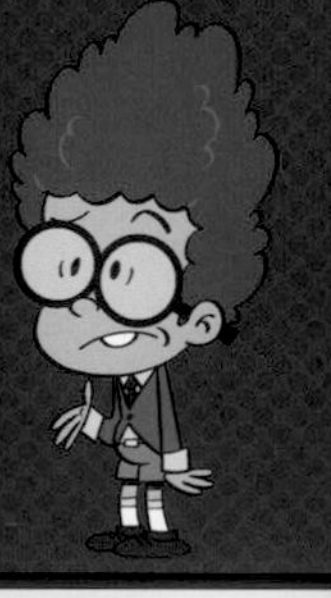

LAIRD

Laird is a total team player and the newest member of Ronnie Anne's friends. Despite often being on the wrong end of misfortune, Laird is an awesome skateboarder who can do tons of tricks…unfortunately stopping is not one of them.

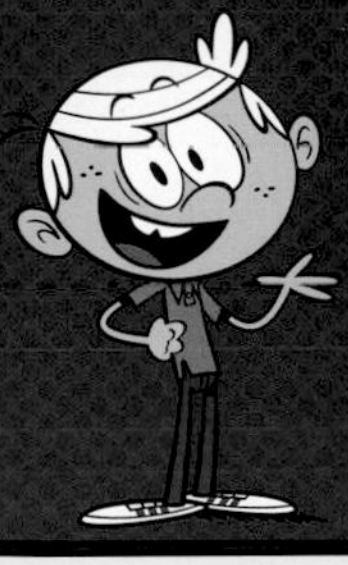

LINCOLN LOUD

Lincoln is Ronnie Anne's dearest friend from Royal Woods. They still keep in touch and visit one another as often as they can. He has learned that surviving the Loud household with ten sisters means staying a step ahead. He's the man with a plan, always coming up with a way to get what he wants or deal with a problem, even if things inevitably go wrong. Lincoln's sisters may drive him crazy, but he loves them and is always willing to help out if they need him.

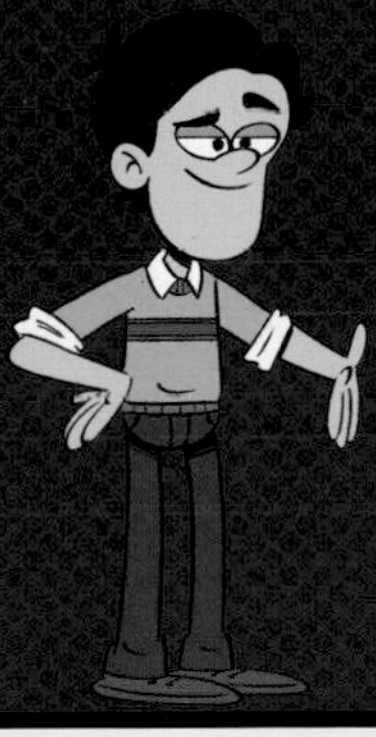

STANLEY CHANG

Stanley Chang is Sid's dad. He's a conductor on the GLART-train that runs through the city. He's a patient man who likes to do Tai Chi when he gets stressed out. He likes to cheer up train commuters with fun facts, but emotionally he breaks down more than the train does.

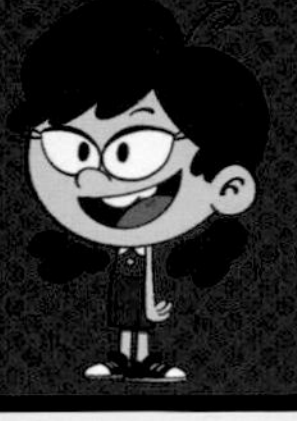

ADELAIDE CHANG

Adelaide Chang is Sid's little sister. She's 6 years old, and has a flair for the dramatic. You can always find her trying to make her way into her big sister Sid's adventures.

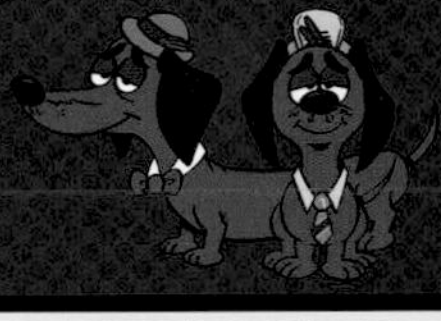

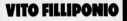

BIG TONY & LITTLE SAL

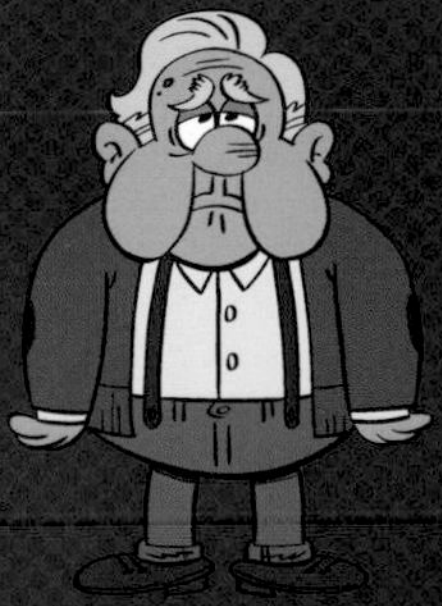

VITO FILLIPONIO

Vito is one of Rosa and Hector's oldest and dearest friends, and a frequent customer at the Mercado. He's lovable, nosy, and usually overstays his welcome, but there is nothing he wouldn't do for his loved ones and his dogs, Big Tony and Little Sal.

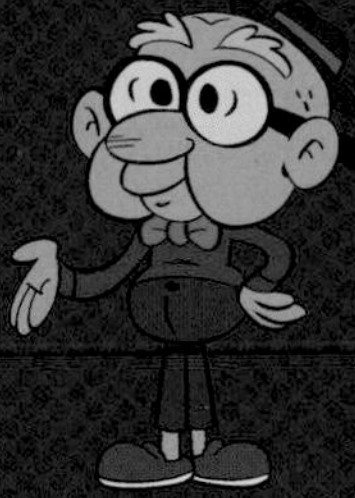

IRVING

Irving is a cheerful, kind old man whom you can usually find sitting on a bench in the park. Irving likes pizza, competing in triathlons, and seeing the best in people, even Carl!

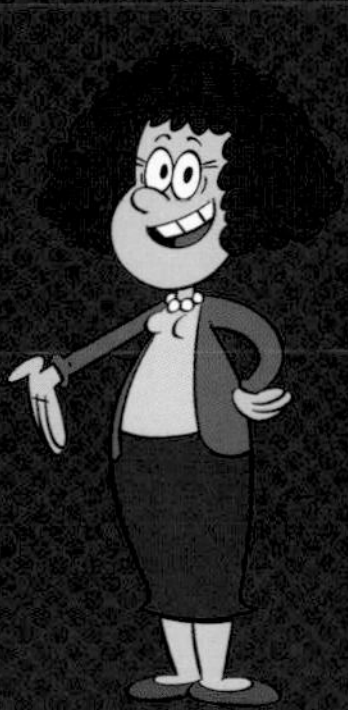

MS GALIANO

Ms. Galiano is Ronnie Anne and the skater kid's teacher at Cesar Chavez Academy. She is sweet as pie and often relies on the kids to keep her up to date on the new, hip, pop culture trends. She briefly dated Ronnie Anne's dad, Arturo, and even though it didn't work out, they still remain friends.

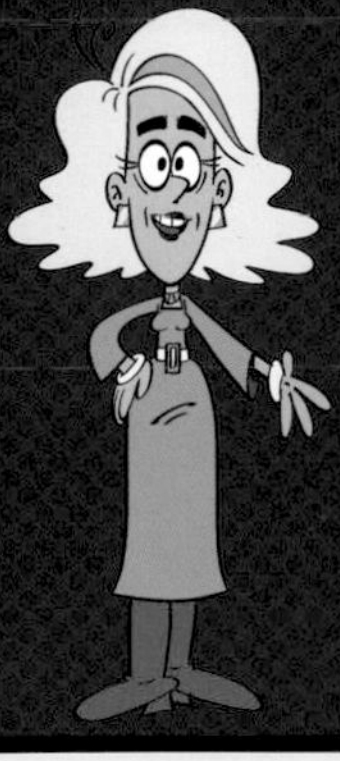

MRS. KERNICKY

Mrs. Kernicky is an Armenian Casagrande neighbor as well as Cesar Chavez Academy's PE teacher and coach. She has a joy and energy for life that is unmatched. Whether she's exercising, competing in dance competitions, or doing an intricate tumbling pass down a GLART train car, it's very unlikely you'd ever find her standing still.

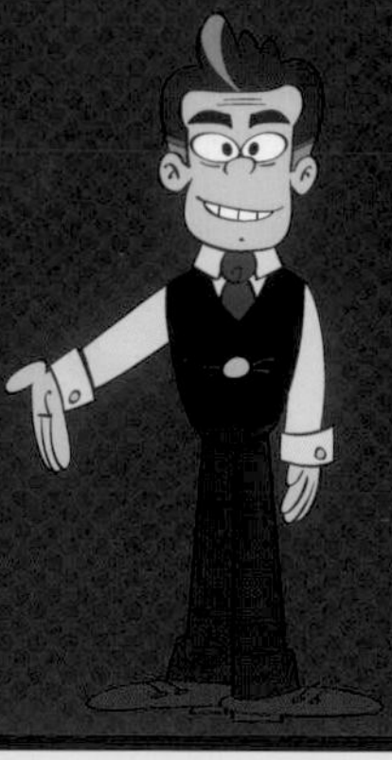

MR. NAKAMURA

Mr. Nakamura is Ronnie Anne's Japanese-American neighbor who lives in an upstairs apartment with his beloved dog, Nelson. He spends much of his time trying to train his perpetually-misbehaving terrier, practicing yoga, and collecting vintage toys. Mr. Nakamura tends to be straight-laced and a bit reserved, but he's nonetheless a kind, conscientious neighbor.

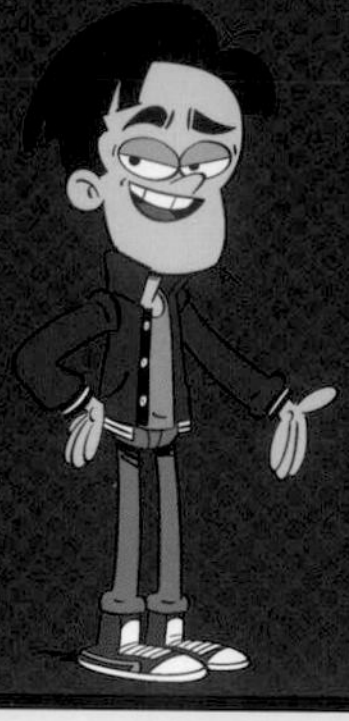

CORY NAKAMURA

Cory is the teenaged son of Mr. Nakamura. He likes playing video games and hanging out at the mercado late when he has insomnia.

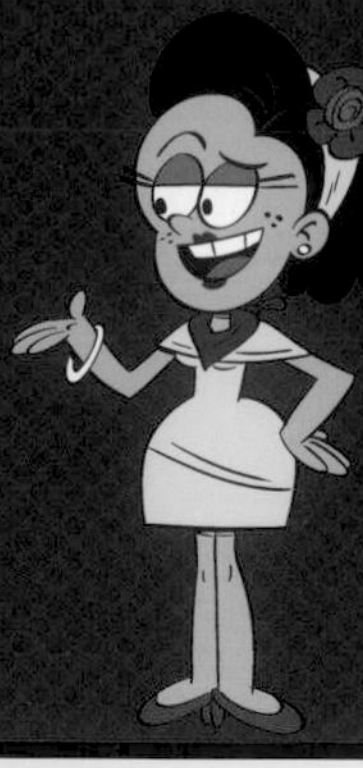

MARGARITA

Margarita is owner and operator of everyone's go-to neighborhood beauty stop, Margarita's Hair Salon. From beautiful blowouts to intricate, towering hair sculptures, she is truly an artist at what she does! Be careful what you reveal to her though, the only thing she likes as a much as styling hair, is talking *chismé* with Hector.

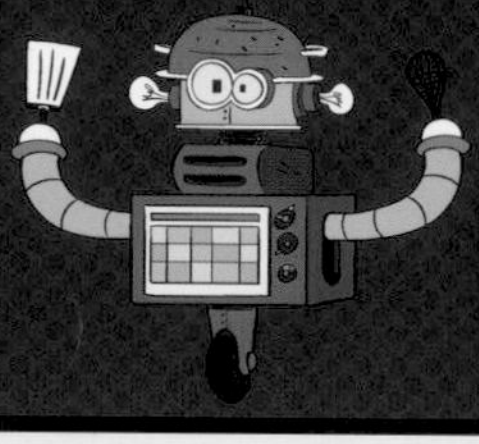

BREAKFAST BOT

Originally built by Sid to help with making breakfast, Breakfast Bot has proven that his capabilities can have multiple functions. He is a team player and always ready to lend a helping hand -- unless it's Sergio that's asking.

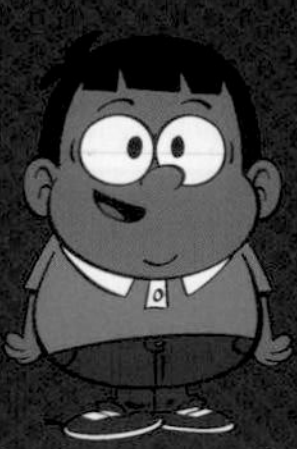

ALEXIS

Mrs. Flores' son, Alexis, is a friendly boy with a big heart. He loves magic, playing the tuba in his school band, and hanging out at the arcade. While he might not be a tough guy, he's a good communicator and he's been known to win over school bullies with hugs. Alexis' family is from El Salvador, and he is a first-generation kid, so he is bilingual as his parents speak primarily Spanish, and also English.

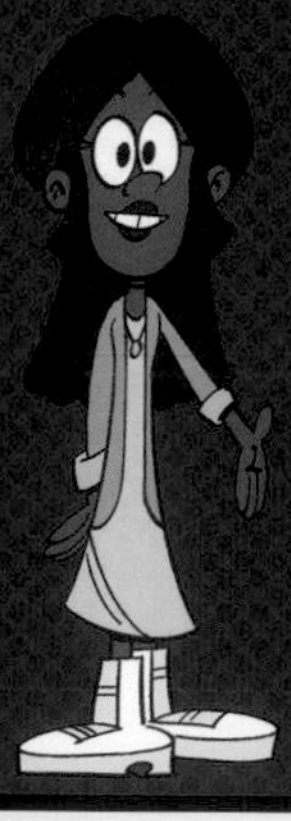

GEORGIA

Georgia lives in apartment 4D of the Casagrande Building with her roommate Miranda. She passes her time by playing cards.

"GODDESS INSPIRED"

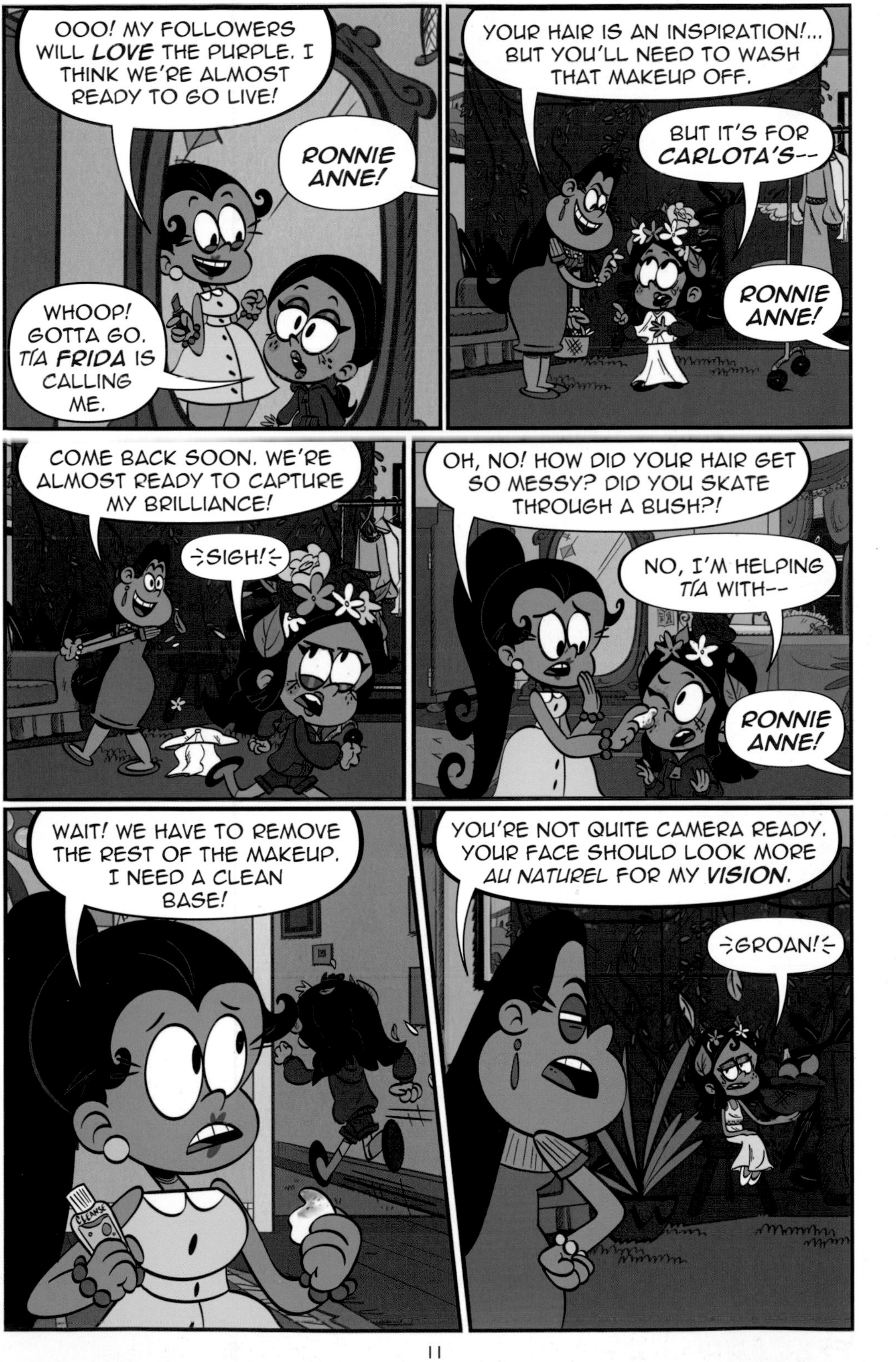

OOO! MY FOLLOWERS WILL *LOVE* THE PURPLE. I THINK WE'RE ALMOST READY TO GO LIVE!
RONNIE ANNE!
WHOOP! GOTTA GO. *TÍA FRIDA* IS CALLING ME.
YOUR HAIR IS AN INSPIRATION!... BUT YOU'LL NEED TO WASH THAT MAKEUP OFF.
BUT IT'S FOR *CARLOTA'S*--
RONNIE ANNE!
COME BACK SOON. WE'RE ALMOST READY TO CAPTURE MY BRILLIANCE!
SIGH!
OH, NO! HOW DID YOUR HAIR GET SO MESSY? DID YOU SKATE THROUGH A BUSH?!
NO, I'M HELPING *TÍA* WITH--
RONNIE ANNE!
WAIT! WE HAVE TO REMOVE THE REST OF THE MAKEUP. I NEED A CLEAN BASE!
CLEANSE
YOU'RE NOT QUITE CAMERA READY. YOUR FACE SHOULD LOOK MORE *AU NATUREL* FOR MY ***VISION***.
GROAN!

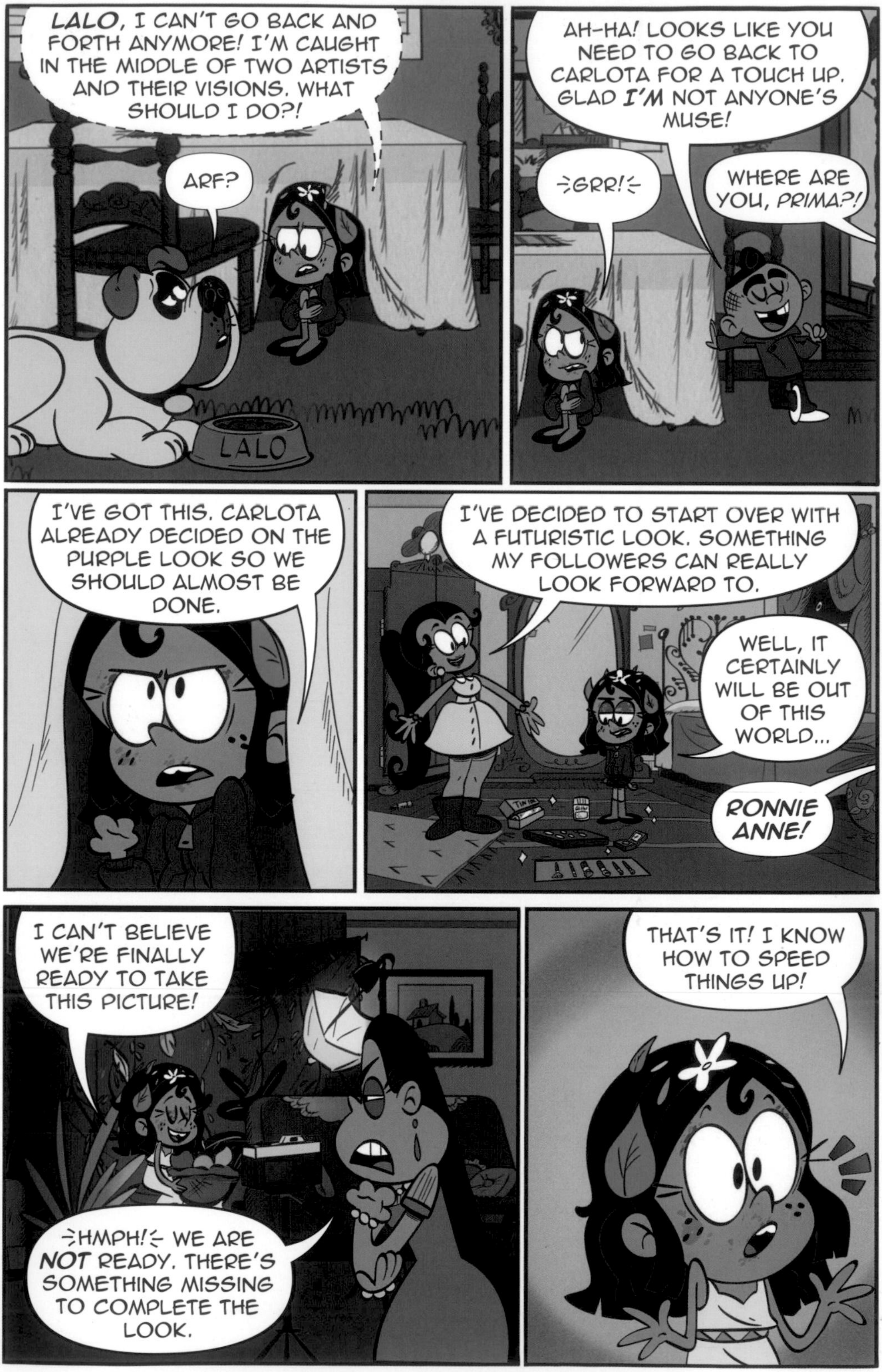
LALO, I CAN'T GO BACK AND FORTH ANYMORE! I'M CAUGHT IN THE MIDDLE OF TWO ARTISTS AND THEIR VISIONS. WHAT SHOULD I DO?!
ARF?
LALO
AH-HA! LOOKS LIKE YOU NEED TO GO BACK TO CARLOTA FOR A TOUCH UP. GLAD I'M NOT ANYONE'S MUSE!
GRR!
WHERE ARE YOU, PRIMA?!
I'VE GOT THIS. CARLOTA ALREADY DECIDED ON THE PURPLE LOOK SO WE SHOULD ALMOST BE DONE.
I'VE DECIDED TO START OVER WITH A FUTURISTIC LOOK. SOMETHING MY FOLLOWERS CAN REALLY LOOK FORWARD TO.
WELL, IT CERTAINLY WILL BE OUT OF THIS WORLD...
RONNIE ANNE!
I CAN'T BELIEVE WE'RE FINALLY READY TO TAKE THIS PICTURE!
HMPH! WE ARE NOT READY. THERE'S SOMETHING MISSING TO COMPLETE THE LOOK.
THAT'S IT! I KNOW HOW TO SPEED THINGS UP!

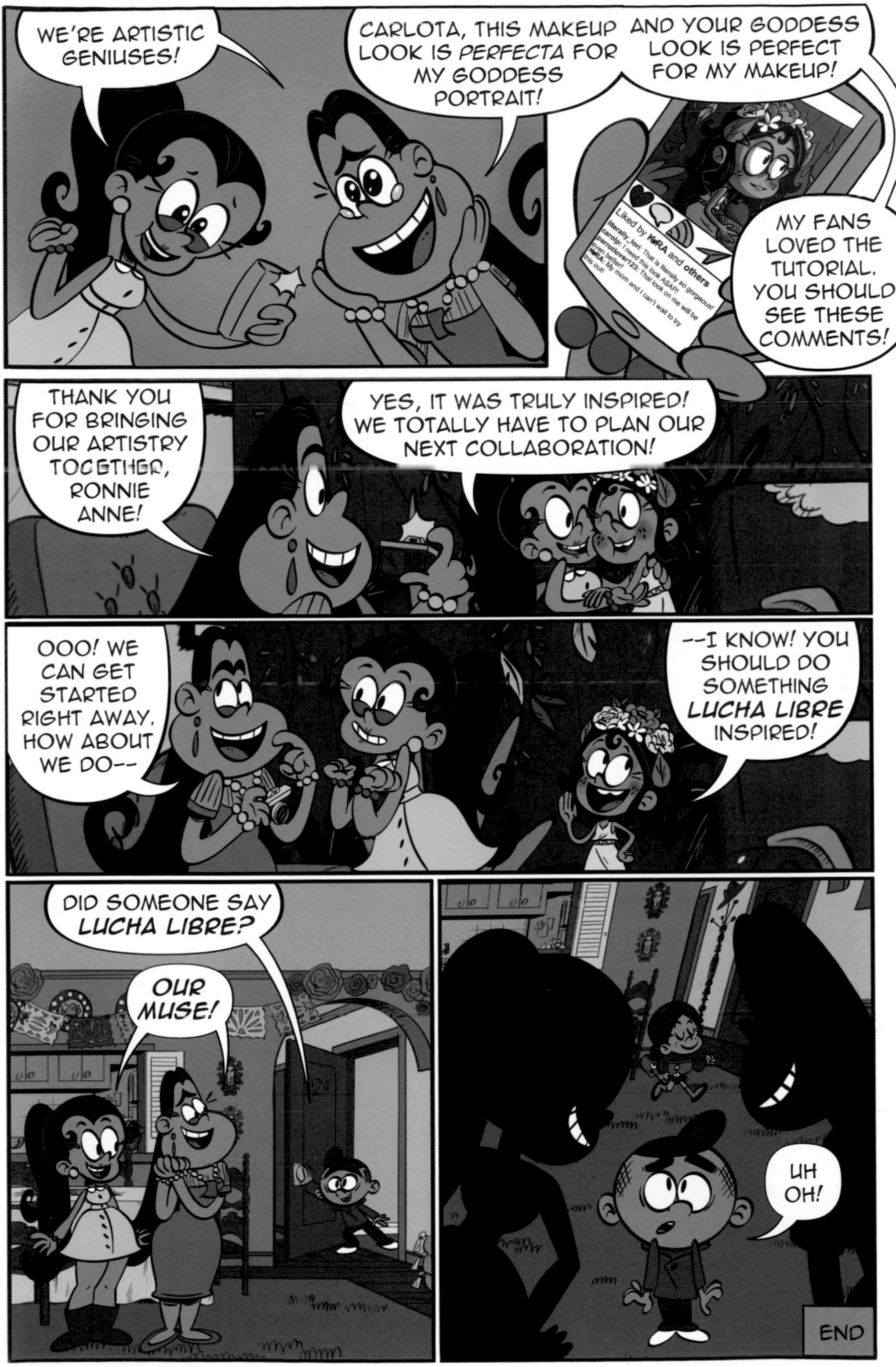

WE'RE ARTISTIC GENIUSES!
CARLOTA, THIS MAKEUP LOOK IS *PERFECTA* FOR MY GODDESS PORTRAIT!
AND YOUR GODDESS LOOK IS PERFECT FOR MY MAKEUP!
Liked by KwRA and others
literally_lori: That is literally so gorgeous!
carolp: I need this look ASAP!
parrotlover123: That look on me will be even better!
KwRA: My mom and I can't wait to try this out!
MY FANS LOVED THE TUTORIAL. YOU SHOULD SEE THESE COMMENTS!
THANK YOU FOR BRINGING OUR ARTISTRY TOGETHER, RONNIE ANNE!
YES, IT WAS TRULY INSPIRED! WE TOTALLY HAVE TO PLAN OUR NEXT COLLABORATION!
OOO! WE CAN GET STARTED RIGHT AWAY. HOW ABOUT WE DO--
--I KNOW! YOU SHOULD DO SOMETHING ***LUCHA LIBRE*** INSPIRED!
DID SOMEONE SAY ***LUCHA LIBRE?***
OUR MUSE!
UH OH!
END

"BARGAIN HUNT"

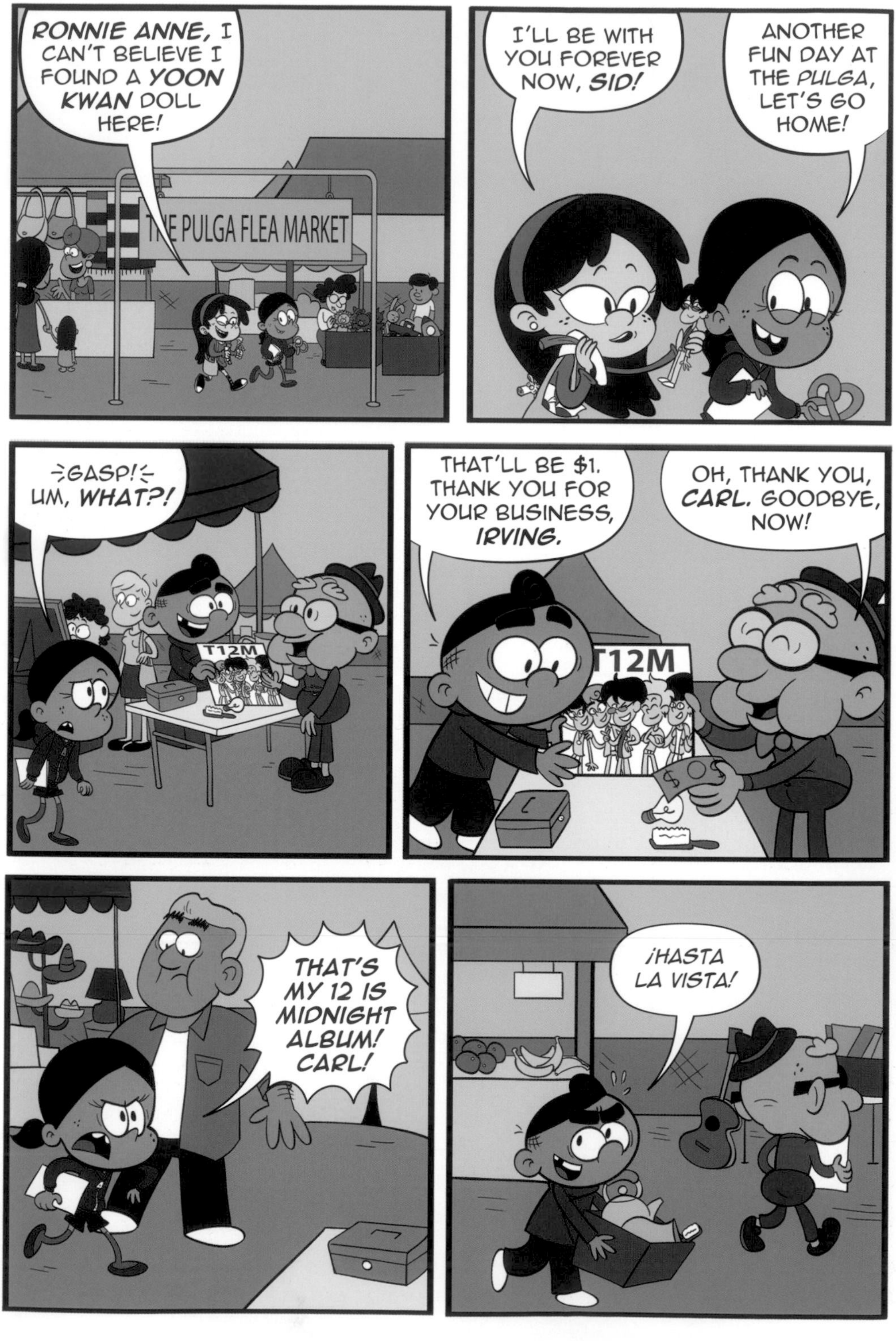
RONNIE ANNE, I CAN'T BELIEVE I FOUND A YOON KWAN DOLL HERE!
THE PULGA FLEA MARKET
I'LL BE WITH YOU FOREVER NOW, SID!
ANOTHER FUN DAY AT THE PULGA, LET'S GO HOME!
GASP! UM, WHAT?!
T12M
THAT'LL BE $1. THANK YOU FOR YOUR BUSINESS, IRVING.
OH, THANK YOU, CARL. GOODBYE, NOW!
T12M
THAT'S MY 12 IS MIDNIGHT ALBUM! CARL!
¡HASTA LA VISTA!

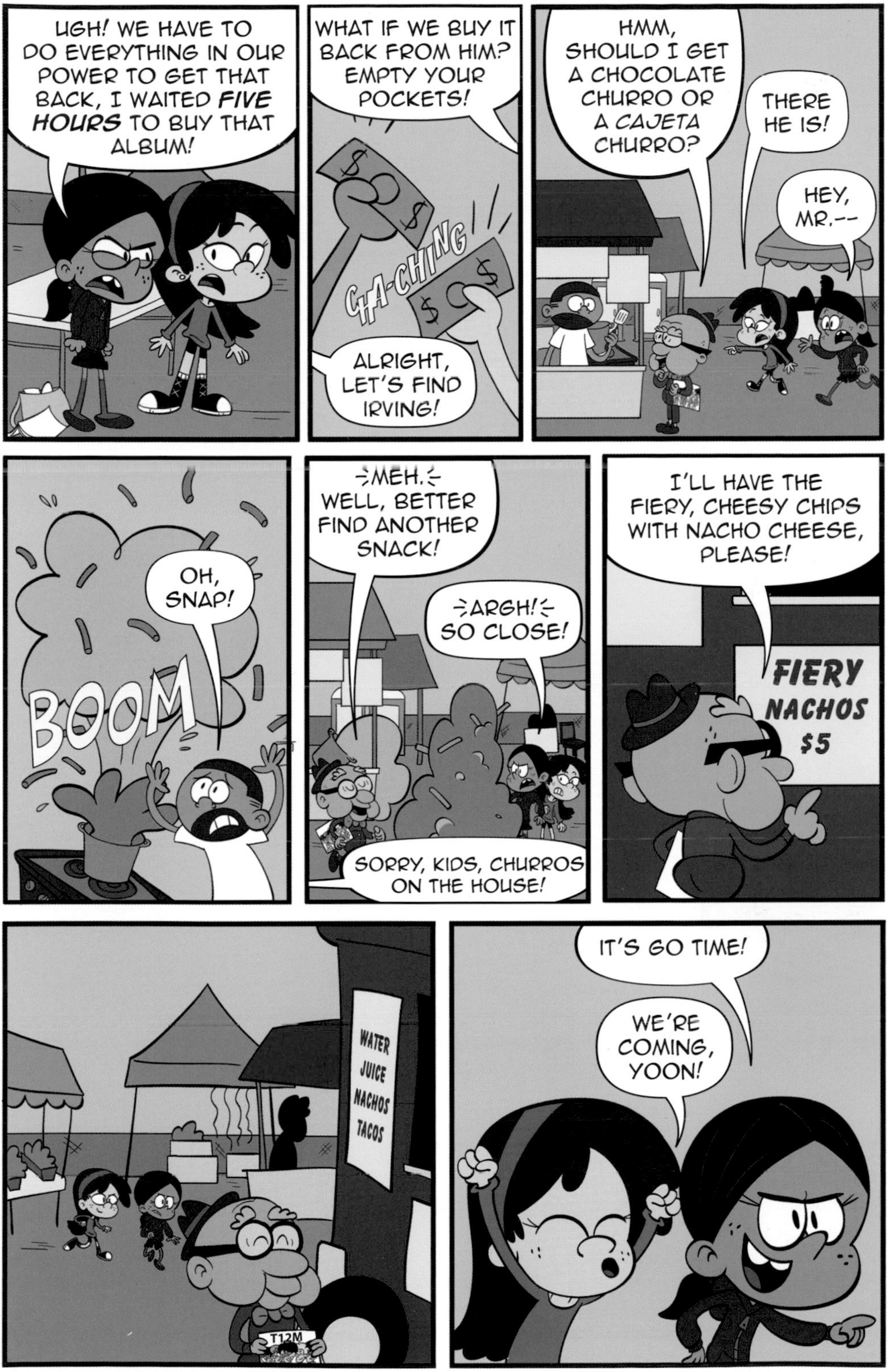

UGH! WE HAVE TO DO EVERYTHING IN OUR POWER TO GET THAT BACK, I WAITED *FIVE HOURS* TO BUY THAT ALBUM!
WHAT IF WE BUY IT BACK FROM HIM? EMPTY YOUR POCKETS!
CHA-CHING
ALRIGHT, LET'S FIND IRVING!
HMM, SHOULD I GET A CHOCOLATE CHURRO OR A *CAJETA* CHURRO?
THERE HE IS!
HEY, MR.--
BOOM
OH, SNAP!
MEH. WELL, BETTER FIND ANOTHER SNACK!
ARGH! SO CLOSE!
SORRY, KIDS, CHURROS ON THE HOUSE!
I'LL HAVE THE FIERY, CHEESY CHIPS WITH NACHO CHEESE, PLEASE!
FIERY NACHOS $5
WATER JUICE NACHOS TACOS
T12M
IT'S GO TIME!
WE'RE COMING, YOON!

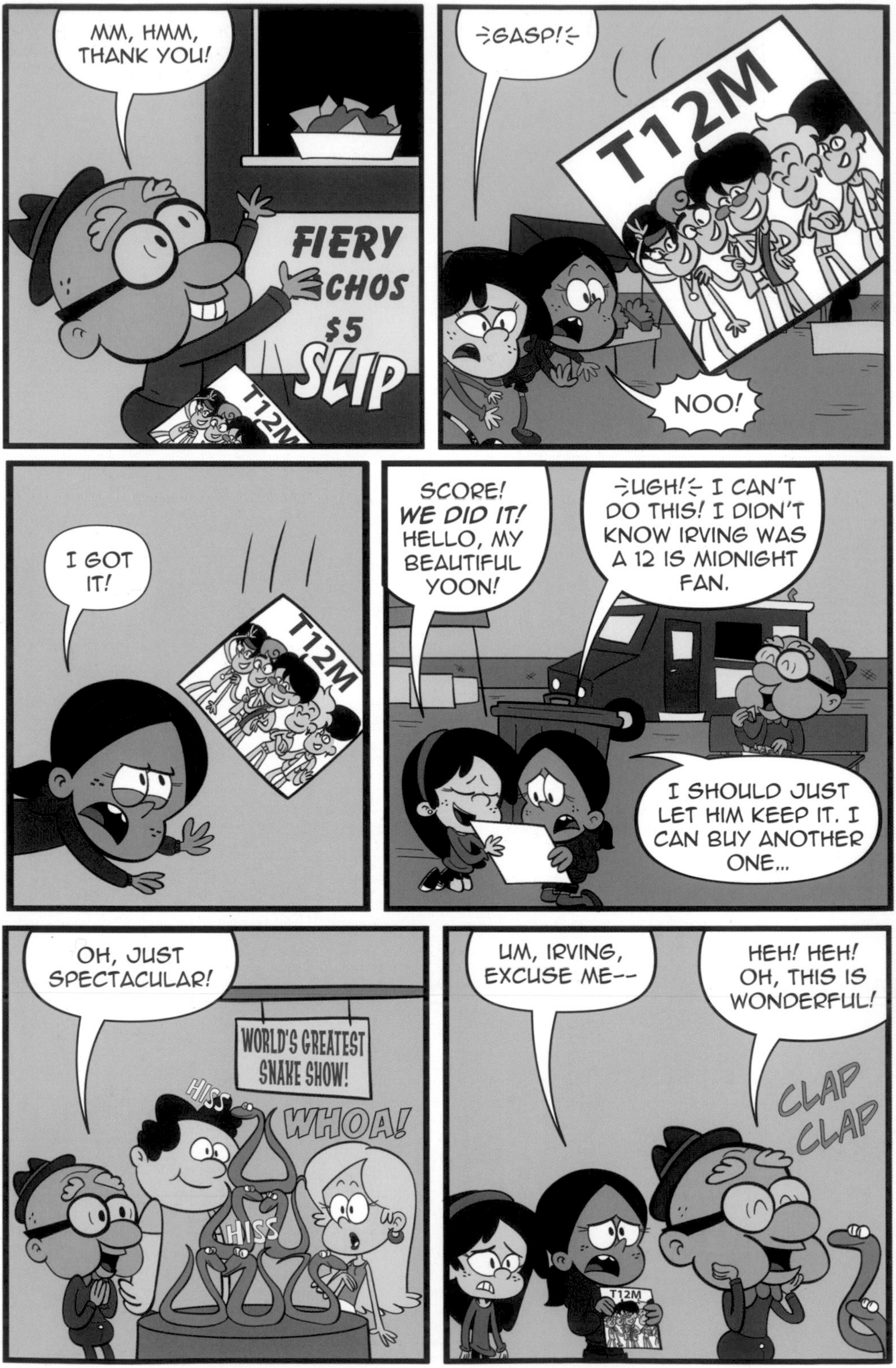
MM, HMM, THANK YOU!
FIERY
CHOS
$5
SLIP
T12M
GASP!
T12M
NOO!
I GOT IT!
T12M
SCORE! *WE DID IT!* HELLO, MY BEAUTIFUL YOON!
UGH! I CAN'T DO THIS! I DIDN'T KNOW IRVING WAS A 12 IS MIDNIGHT FAN.
I SHOULD JUST LET HIM KEEP IT. I CAN BUY ANOTHER ONE...
OH, JUST SPECTACULAR!
WORLD'S GREATEST SNAKE SHOW!
HISS
WHOA!
HISS
UM, IRVING, EXCUSE ME--
HEH! HEH! OH, THIS IS WONDERFUL!
CLAP
CLAP
T12M

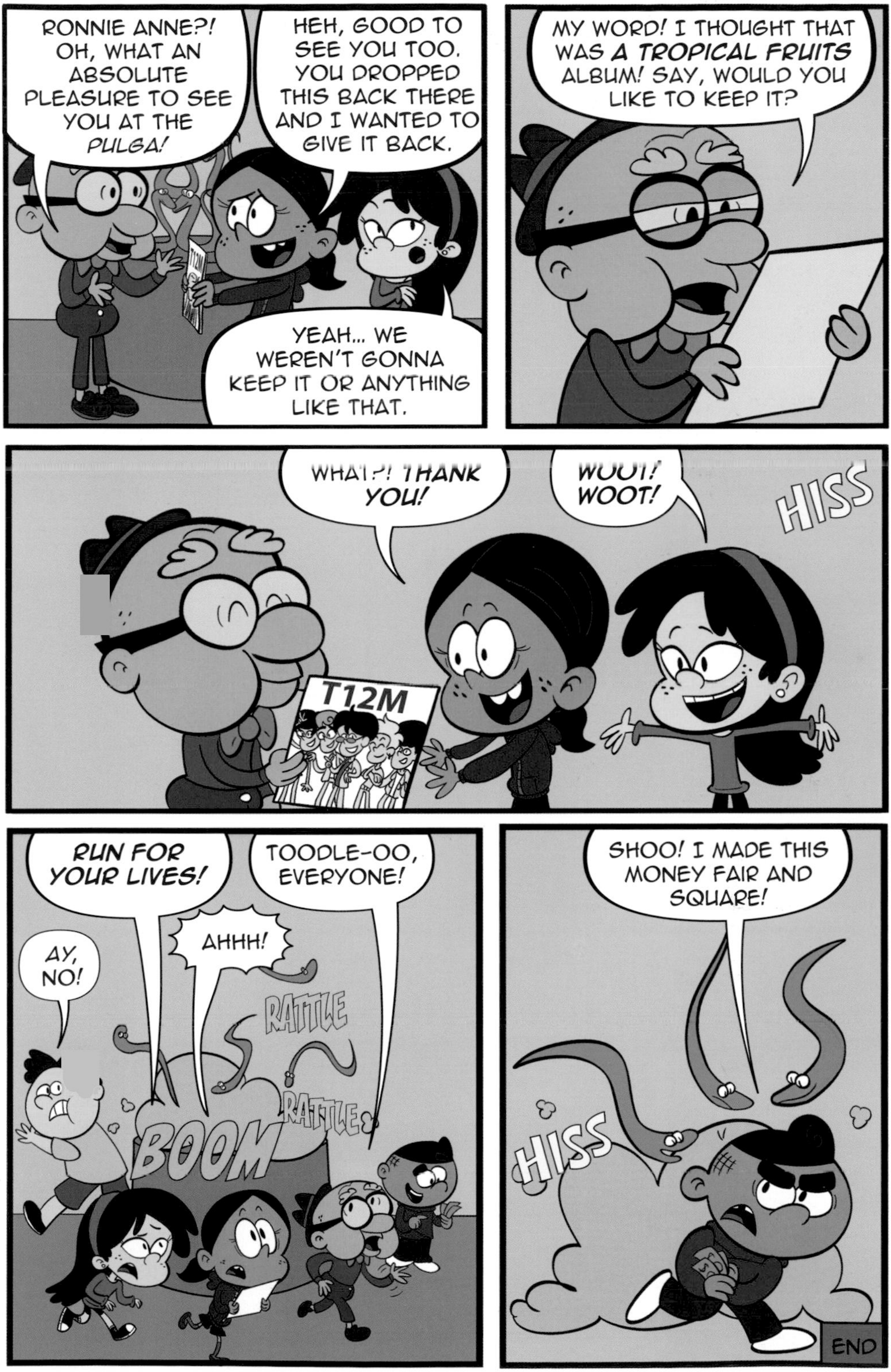

RONNIE ANNE?! OH, WHAT AN ABSOLUTE PLEASURE TO SEE YOU AT THE *PULGA!*
HEH, GOOD TO SEE YOU TOO. YOU DROPPED THIS BACK THERE AND I WANTED TO GIVE IT BACK.
T12M
YEAH... WE WEREN'T GONNA KEEP IT OR ANYTHING LIKE THAT.
MY WORD! I THOUGHT THAT WAS ***A TROPICAL FRUITS*** ALBUM! SAY, WOULD YOU LIKE TO KEEP IT?
WHAT?! ***THANK YOU!***
WOOT! WOOT!
HISS
T12M
RUN FOR YOUR LIVES!
TOODLE-OO, EVERYONE!
AY, NO!
AHHH!
RATTLE
RATTLE
BOOM
SHOO! I MADE THIS MONEY FAIR AND SQUARE!
HISS
END

"POP UP"

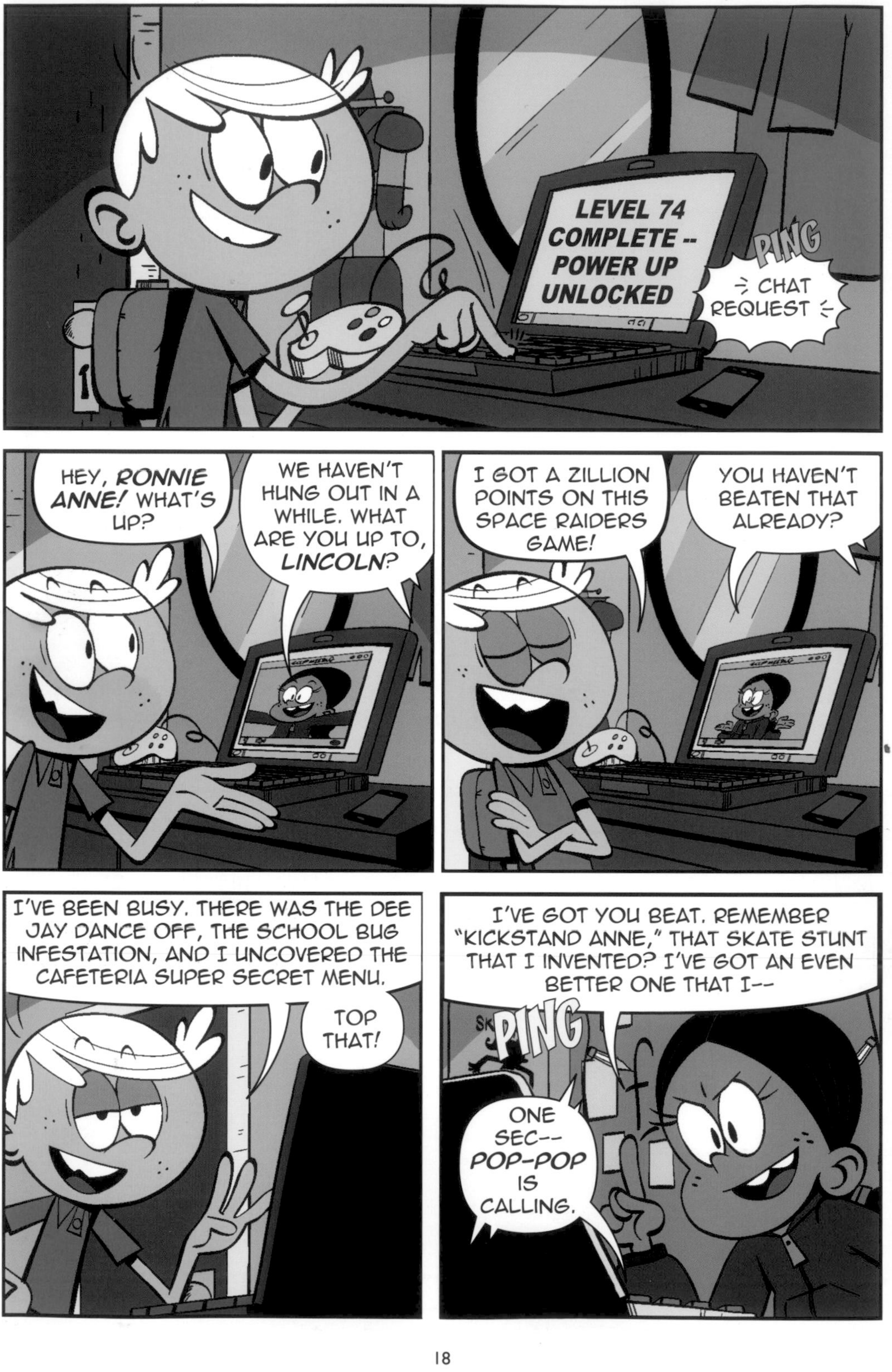
LEVEL 74 COMPLETE -- POWER UP UNLOCKED
PING
CHAT REQUEST
HEY, RONNIE ANNE! WHAT'S UP?
WE HAVEN'T HUNG OUT IN A WHILE. WHAT ARE YOU UP TO, LINCOLN?
I GOT A ZILLION POINTS ON THIS SPACE RAIDERS GAME!
YOU HAVEN'T BEATEN THAT ALREADY?
I'VE BEEN BUSY. THERE WAS THE DEE JAY DANCE OFF, THE SCHOOL BUG INFESTATION, AND I UNCOVERED THE CAFETERIA SUPER SECRET MENU.
TOP THAT!
I'VE GOT YOU BEAT. REMEMBER "KICKSTAND ANNE," THAT SKATE STUNT THAT I INVENTED? I'VE GOT AN EVEN BETTER ONE THAT I--
PING
ONE SEC-- POP-POP IS CALLING.

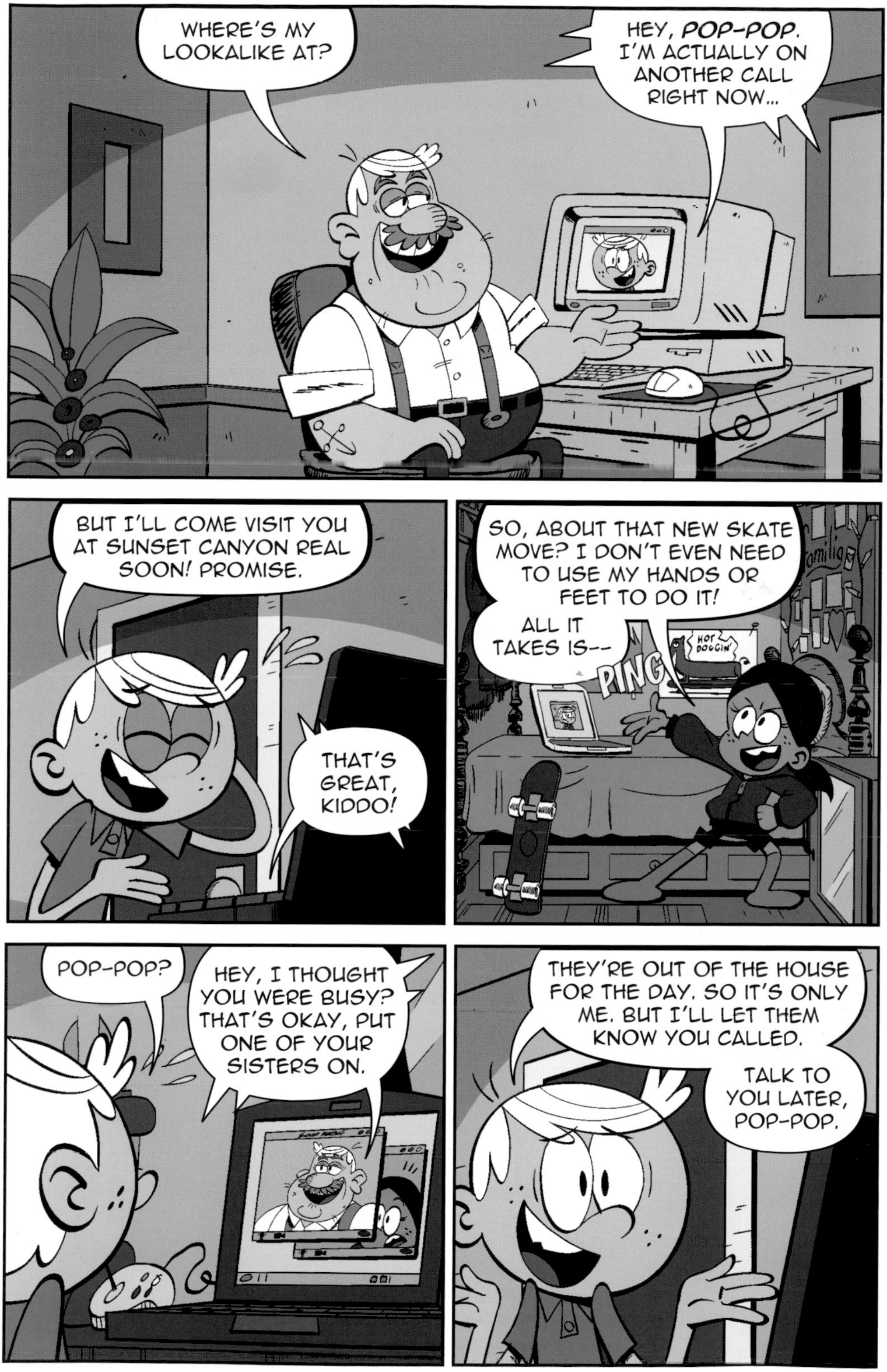
WHERE'S MY LOOKALIKE AT?
HEY, POP-POP. I'M ACTUALLY ON ANOTHER CALL RIGHT NOW...
BUT I'LL COME VISIT YOU AT SUNSET CANYON REAL SOON! PROMISE.
THAT'S GREAT, KIDDO!
SO, ABOUT THAT NEW SKATE MOVE? I DON'T EVEN NEED TO USE MY HANDS OR FEET TO DO IT!
ALL IT TAKES IS--
PING
HOT DOGGIN'
POP-POP?
HEY, I THOUGHT YOU WERE BUSY? THAT'S OKAY, PUT ONE OF YOUR SISTERS ON.
THEY'RE OUT OF THE HOUSE FOR THE DAY. SO IT'S ONLY ME. BUT I'LL LET THEM KNOW YOU CALLED.
TALK TO YOU LATER, POP-POP.

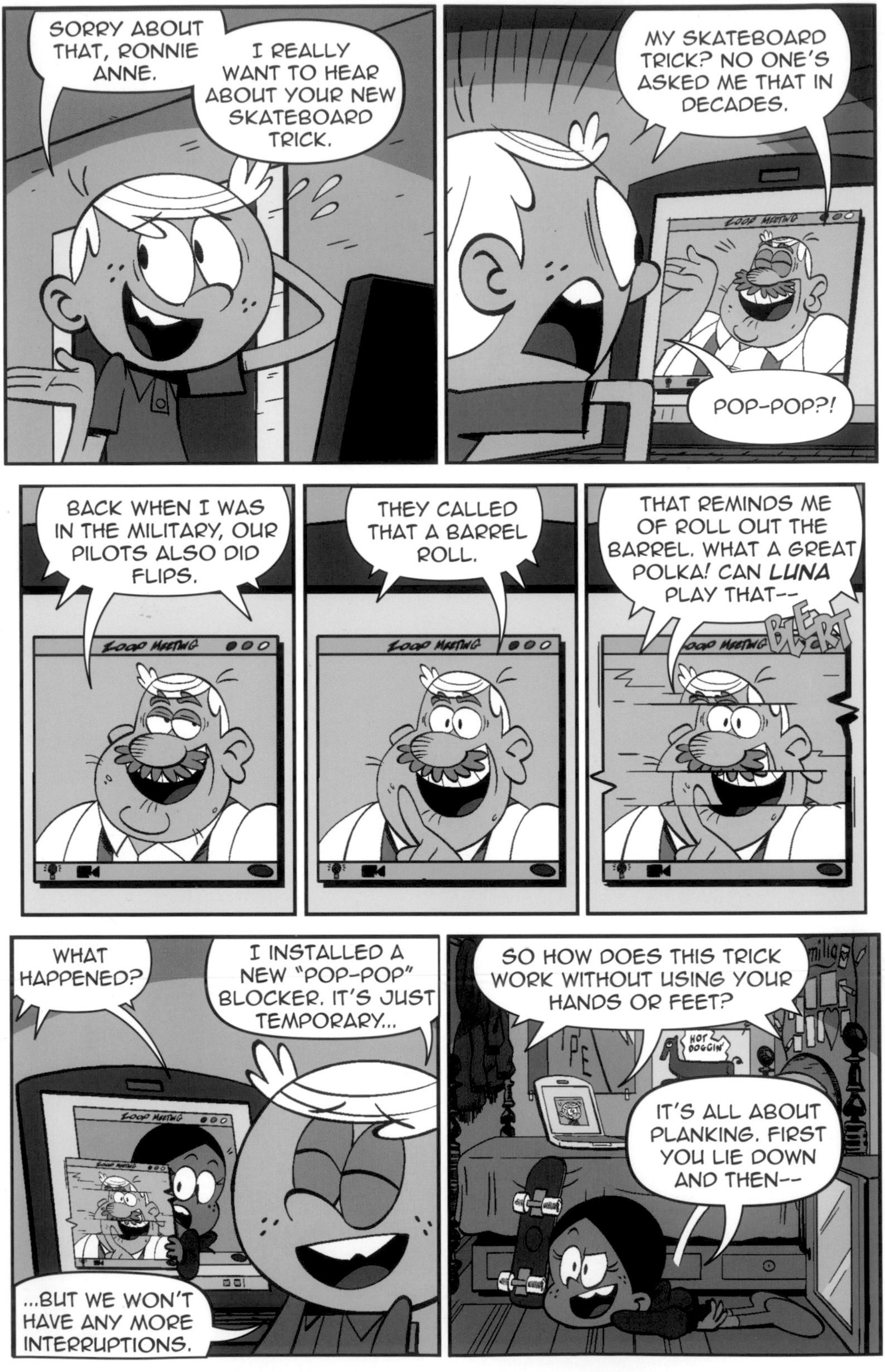
SORRY ABOUT THAT, RONNIE ANNE.
I REALLY WANT TO HEAR ABOUT YOUR NEW SKATEBOARD TRICK.
MY SKATEBOARD TRICK? NO ONE'S ASKED ME THAT IN DECADES.
POP-POP?!
BACK WHEN I WAS IN THE MILITARY, OUR PILOTS ALSO DID FLIPS.
THEY CALLED THAT A BARREL ROLL.
THAT REMINDS ME OF ROLL OUT THE BARREL. WHAT A GREAT POLKA! CAN LUNA PLAY THAT--
BLERT
WHAT HAPPENED?
I INSTALLED A NEW "POP-POP" BLOCKER. IT'S JUST TEMPORARY...
...BUT WE WON'T HAVE ANY MORE INTERRUPTIONS.
SO HOW DOES THIS TRICK WORK WITHOUT USING YOUR HANDS OR FEET?
HOT DOGGIN'
IT'S ALL ABOUT PLANKING. FIRST YOU LIE DOWN AND THEN--

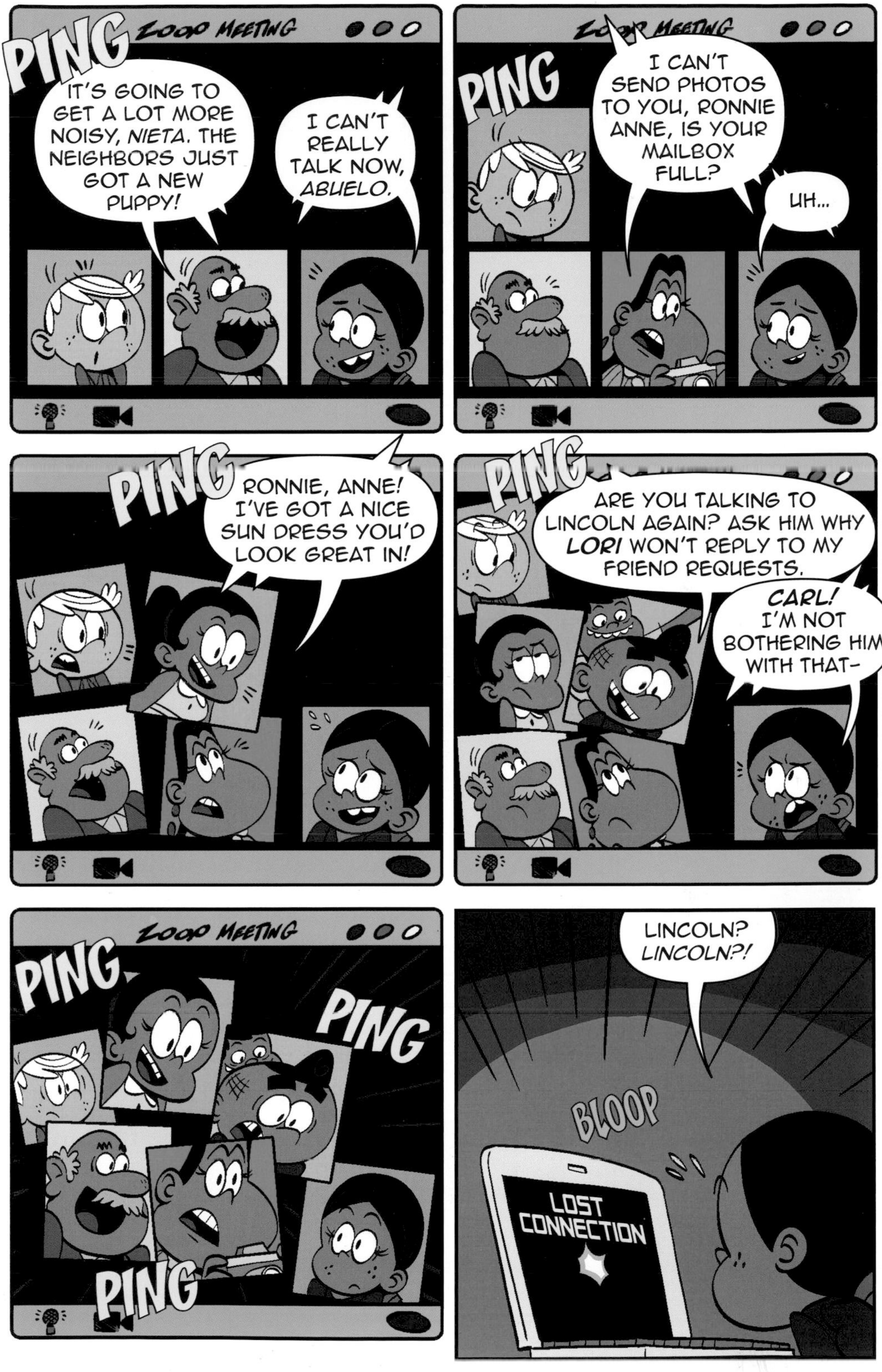
ZOOP MEETING
PING
IT'S GOING TO GET A LOT MORE NOISY, NIETA. THE NEIGHBORS JUST GOT A NEW PUPPY!
I CAN'T REALLY TALK NOW, ABUELO.
ZOOP MEETING
PING
I CAN'T SEND PHOTOS TO YOU, RONNIE ANNE, IS YOUR MAILBOX FULL?
UH...
PING
RONNIE, ANNE! I'VE GOT A NICE SUN DRESS YOU'D LOOK GREAT IN!
PING
ARE YOU TALKING TO LINCOLN AGAIN? ASK HIM WHY LORI WON'T REPLY TO MY FRIEND REQUESTS.
CARL! I'M NOT BOTHERING HIM WITH THAT-
ZOOP MEETING
PING
PING
PING
LINCOLN? LINCOLN?!
BLOOP
LOST CONNECTION

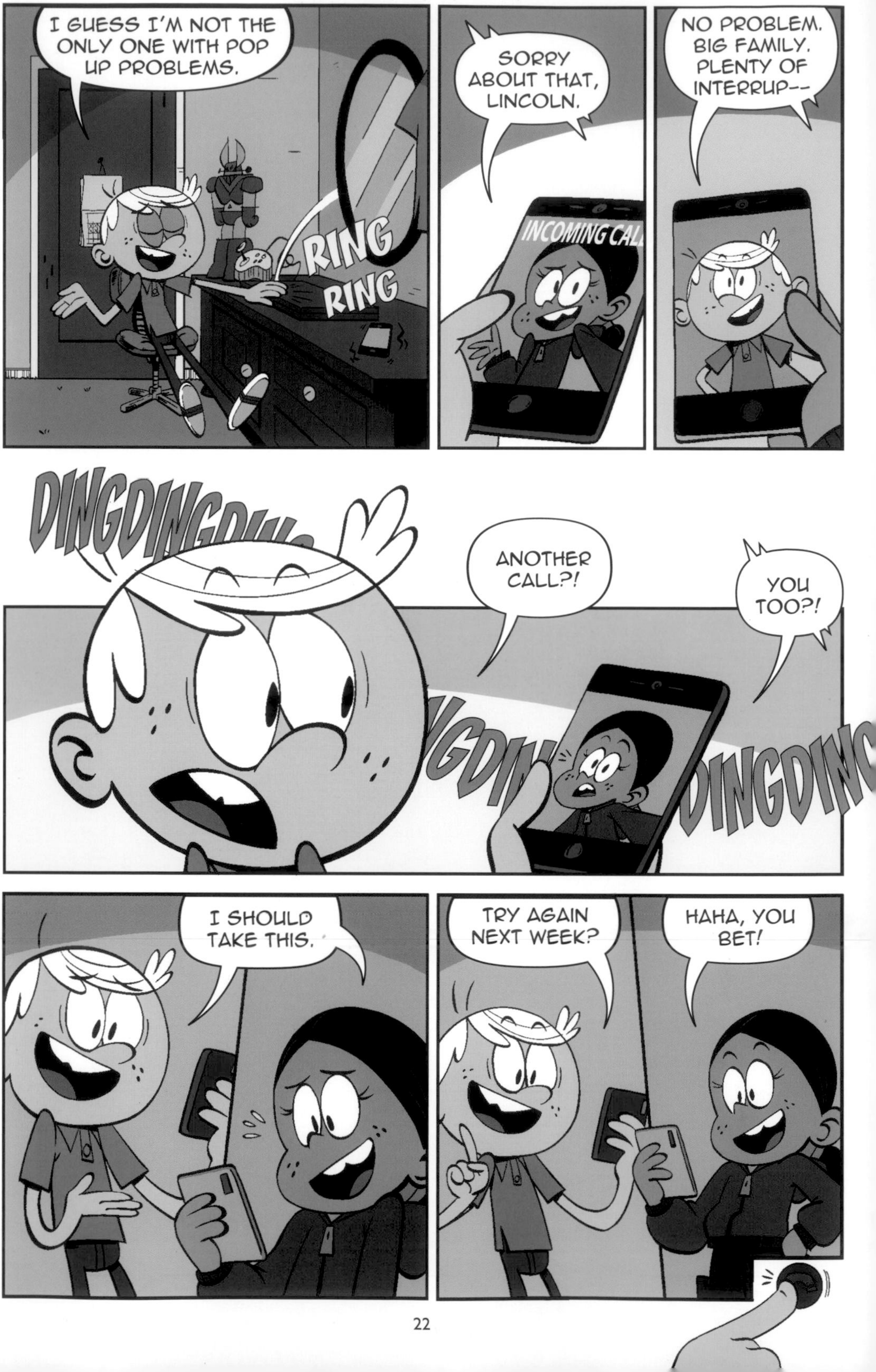
I GUESS I'M NOT THE ONLY ONE WITH POP UP PROBLEMS.
RING
RING
SORRY ABOUT THAT, LINCOLN.
INCOMING CALL
NO PROBLEM. BIG FAMILY. PLENTY OF INTERRUP--
DINGDINGDING
ANOTHER CALL?!
YOU TOO?!
DINGDING
I SHOULD TAKE THIS.
TRY AGAIN NEXT WEEK?
HAHA, YOU BET!

"TUBADOUR"

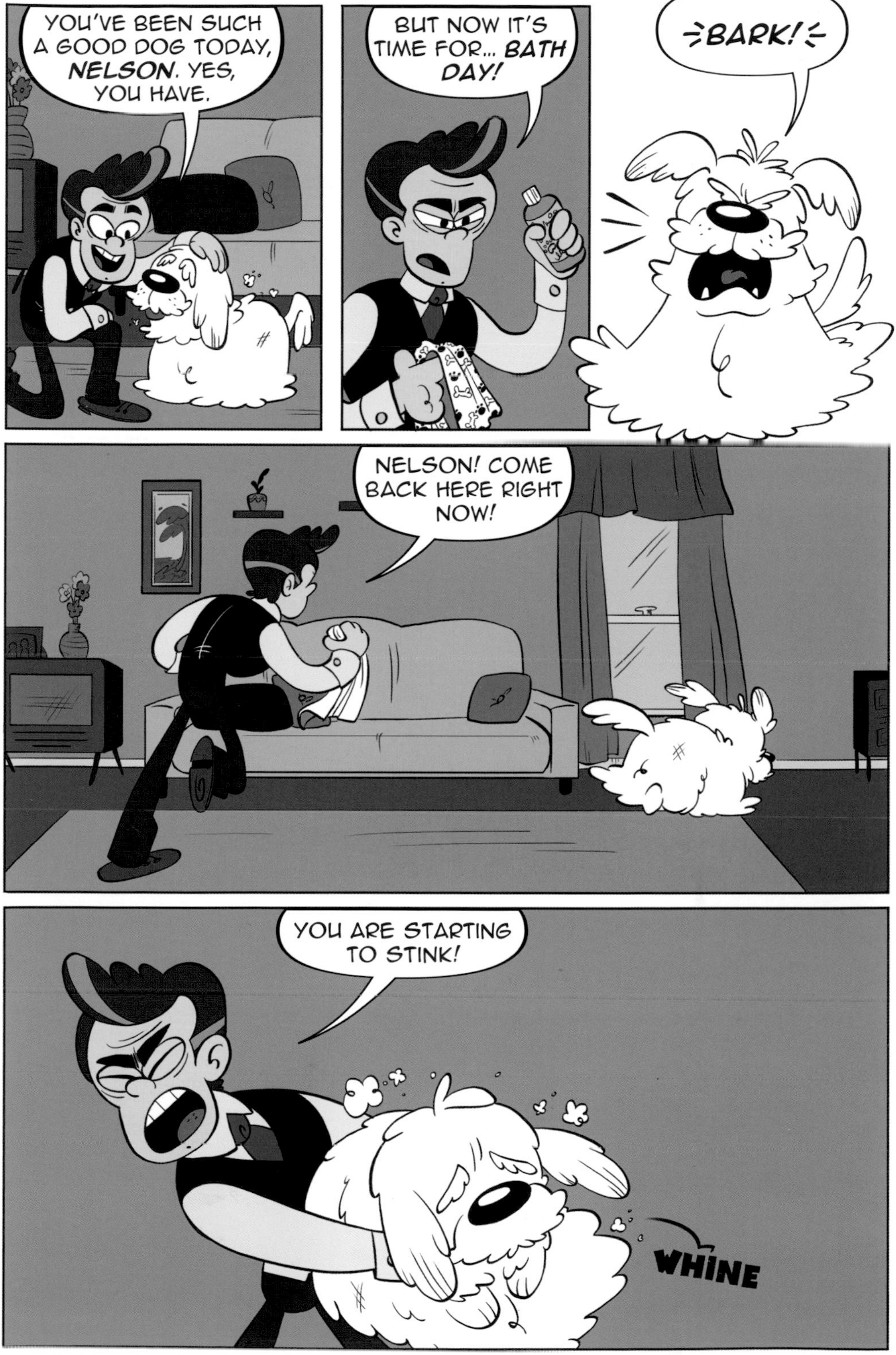

YOU'VE BEEN SUCH A GOOD DOG TODAY, NELSON. YES, YOU HAVE.
BUT NOW IT'S TIME FOR... BATH DAY!
BARK!
NELSON! COME BACK HERE RIGHT NOW!
YOU ARE STARTING TO STINK!
WHINE

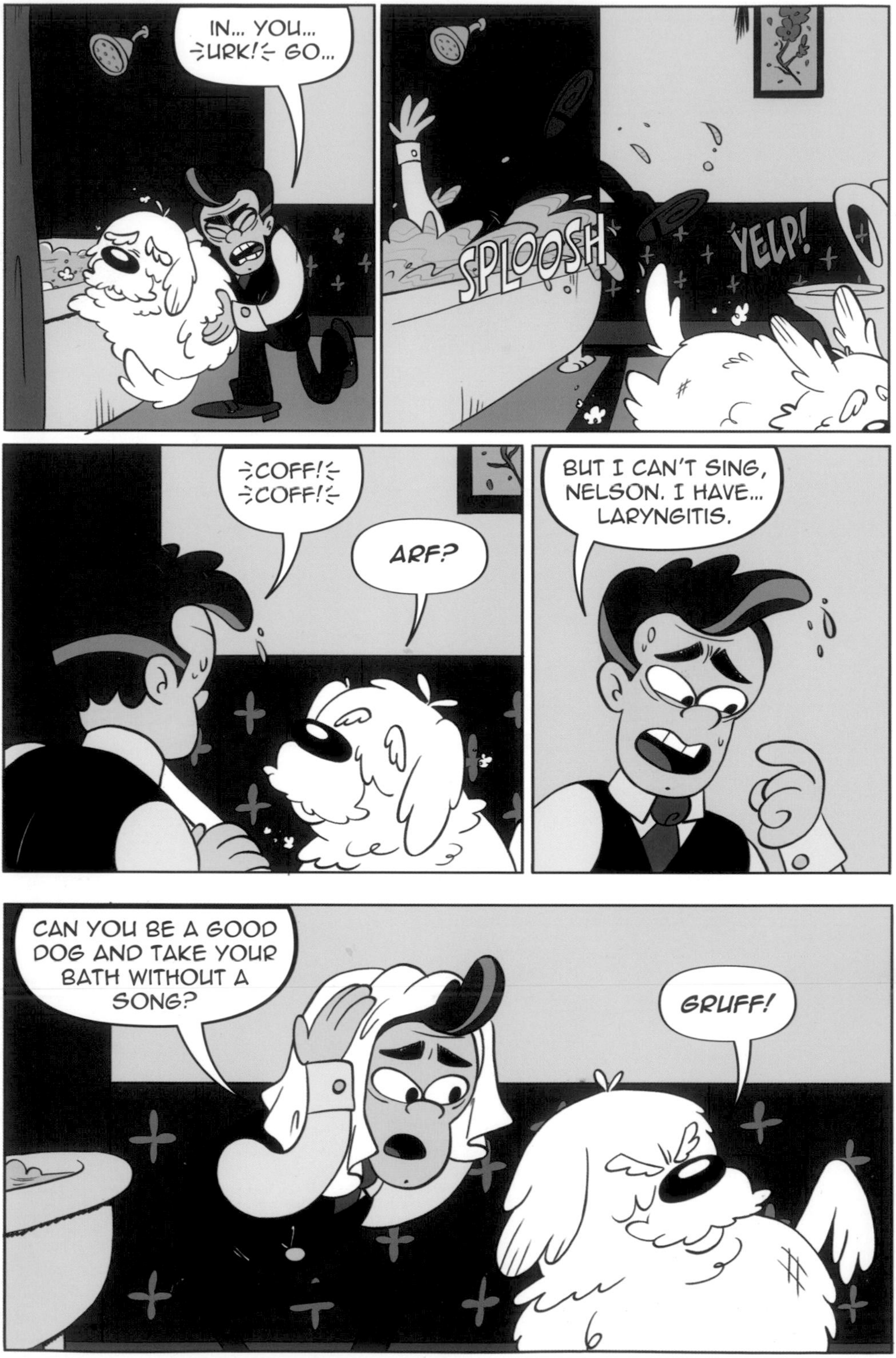
IN... YOU... ⁼URK!⁼ GO...
SPLOOSH
YELP!
⁼COFF!⁼ ⁼COFF!⁼
ARF?
BUT I CAN'T SING, NELSON. I HAVE... LARYNGITIS.
CAN YOU BE A GOOD DOG AND TAKE YOUR BATH WITHOUT A SONG?
GRUFF!

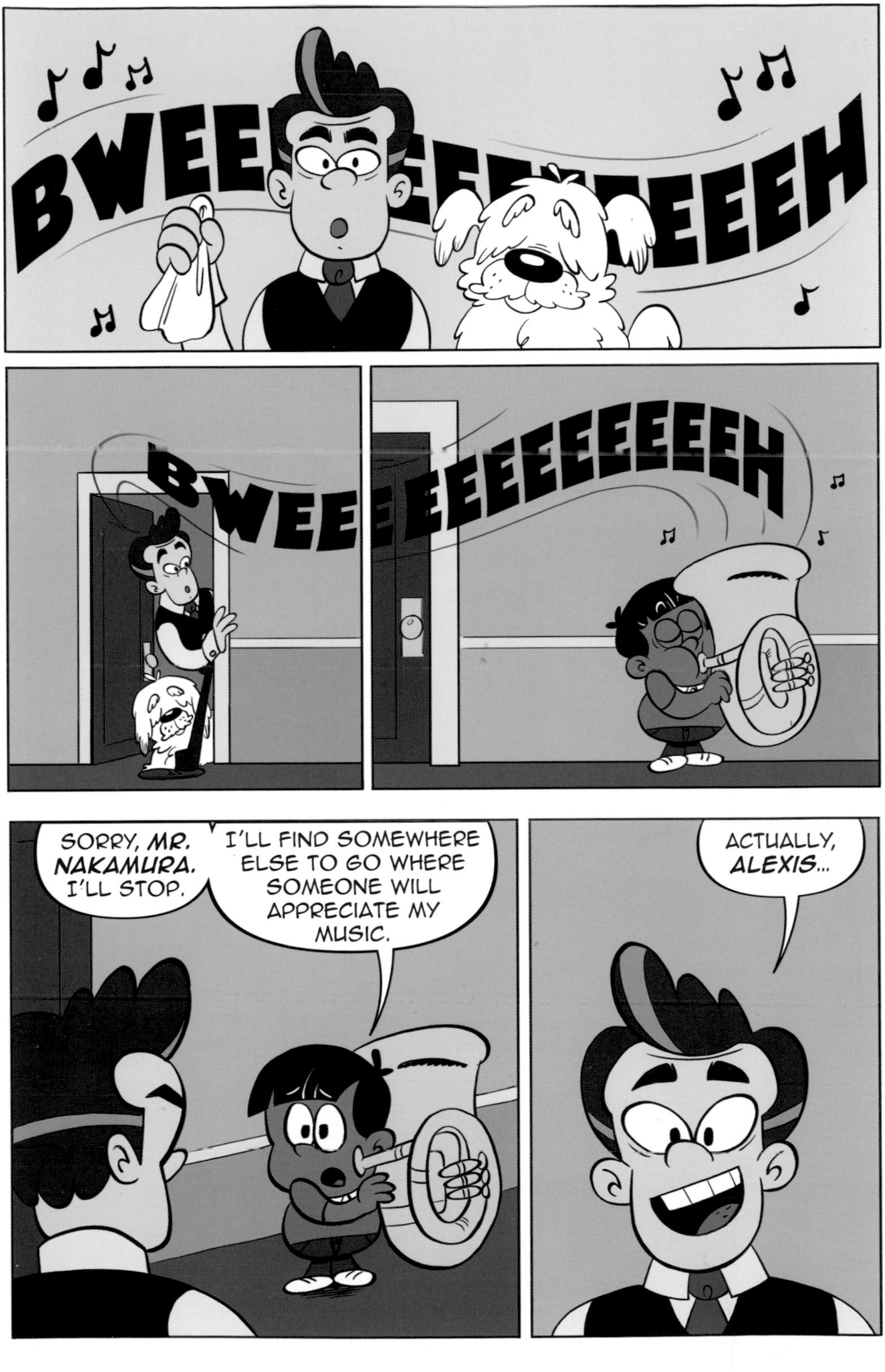
BWEEEEEEEEEEEEH
BWEEEEEEEEEEEEH
SORRY, MR. NAKAMURA. I'LL STOP.
I'LL FIND SOMEWHERE ELSE TO GO WHERE SOMEONE WILL APPRECIATE MY MUSIC.
ACTUALLY, ALEXIS...

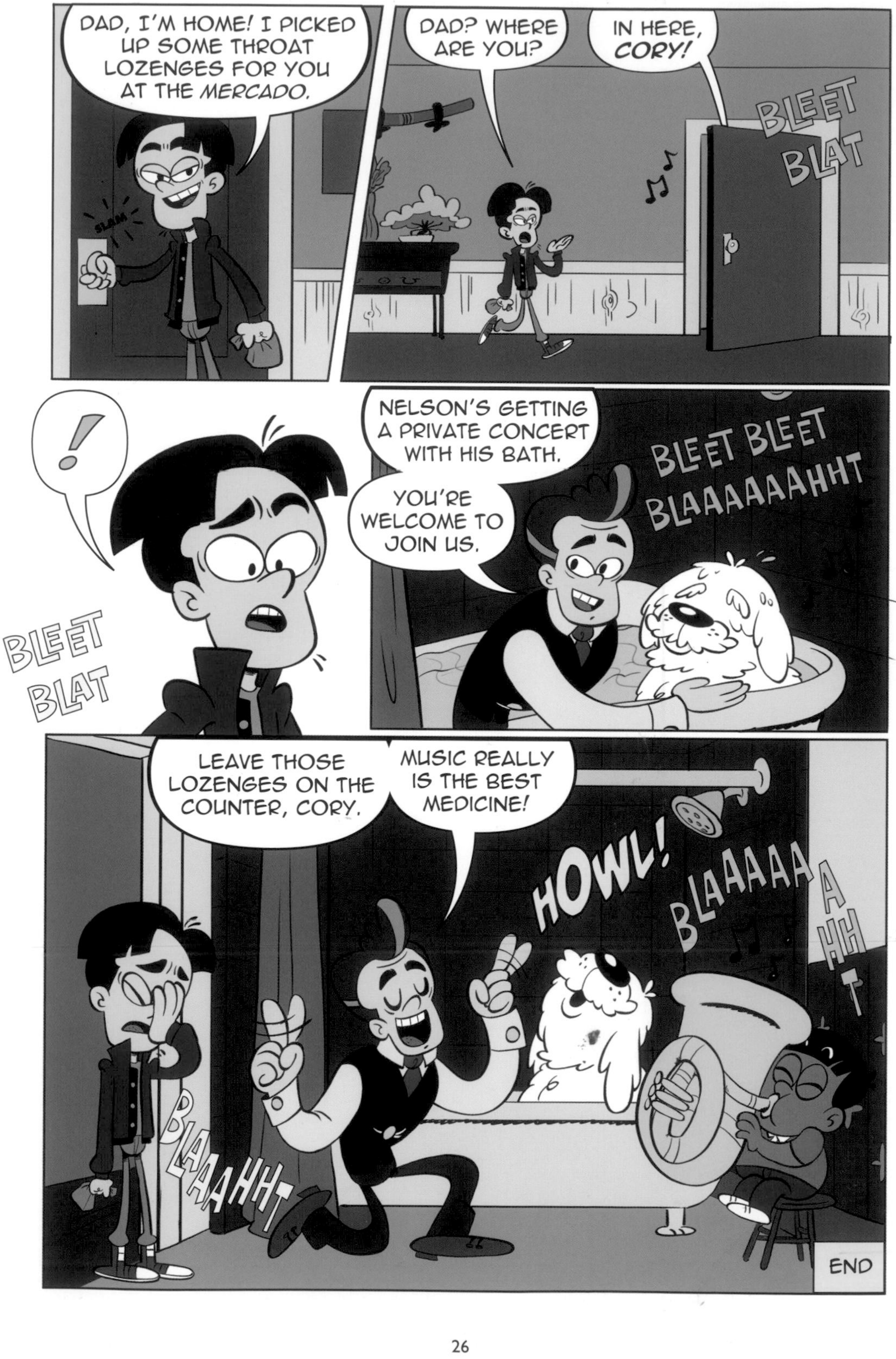
DAD, I'M HOME! I PICKED UP SOME THROAT LOZENGES FOR YOU AT THE *MERCADO*.
SLAM
DAD? WHERE ARE YOU?
IN HERE, *CORY!*
BLEET
BLAT
!
BLEET
BLAT
NELSON'S GETTING A PRIVATE CONCERT WITH HIS BATH.
YOU'RE WELCOME TO JOIN US.
BLEET BLEET
BLAAAAAAHHT
LEAVE THOSE LOZENGES ON THE COUNTER, CORY.
MUSIC REALLY IS THE BEST MEDICINE!
HOWL!
BLAAAAAAHHT
BLAAAHHT
END

"HUNT FROM HOME"

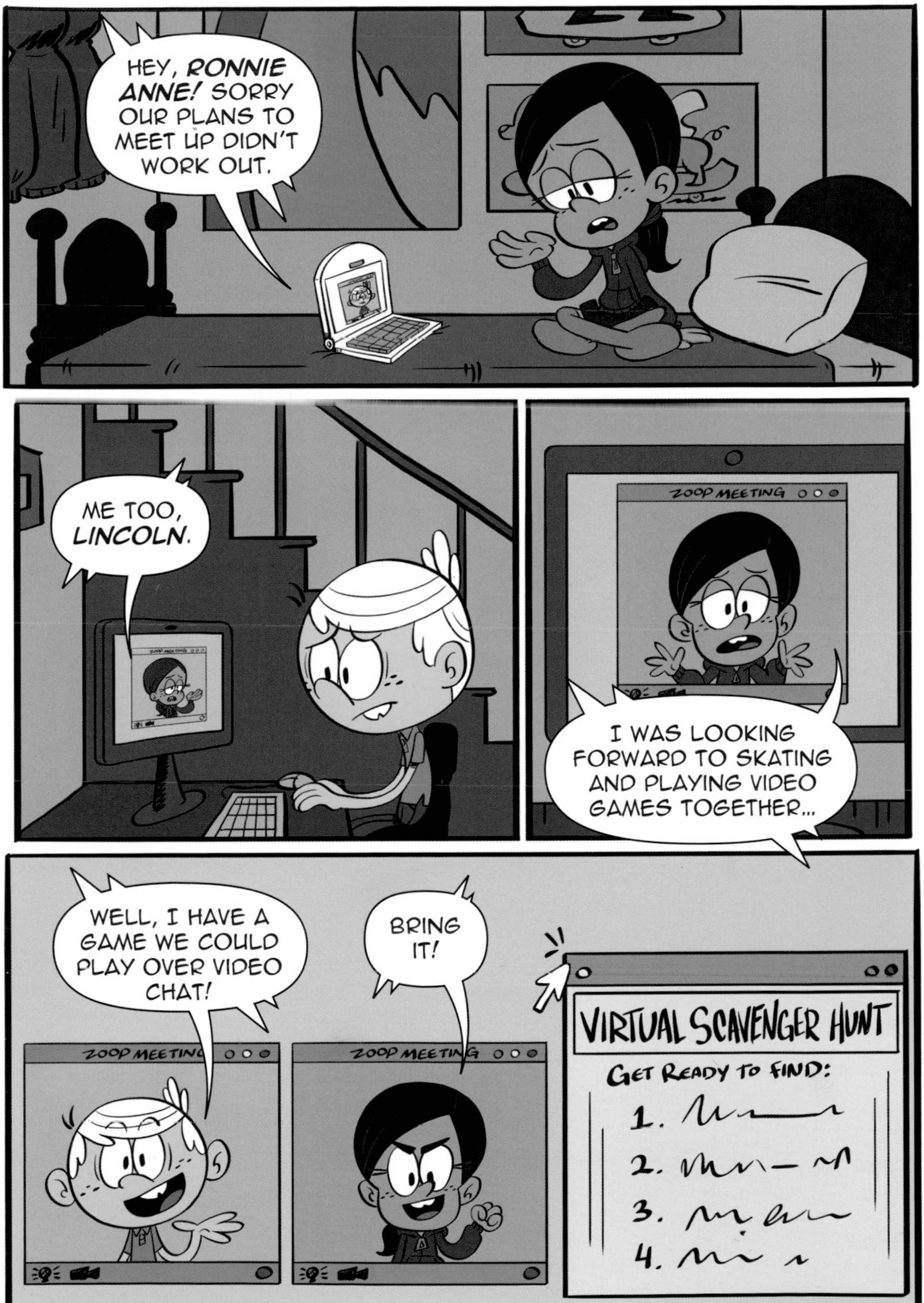
HEY, RONNIE ANNE! SORRY OUR PLANS TO MEET UP DIDN'T WORK OUT.
ME TOO, LINCOLN.
ZOOP MEETING
I WAS LOOKING FORWARD TO SKATING AND PLAYING VIDEO GAMES TOGETHER...
WELL, I HAVE A GAME WE COULD PLAY OVER VIDEO CHAT!
BRING IT!
ZOOP MEETING
ZOOP MEETING
VIRTUAL SCAVENGER HUNT
GET READY TO FIND:
1.
2.
3.
4.

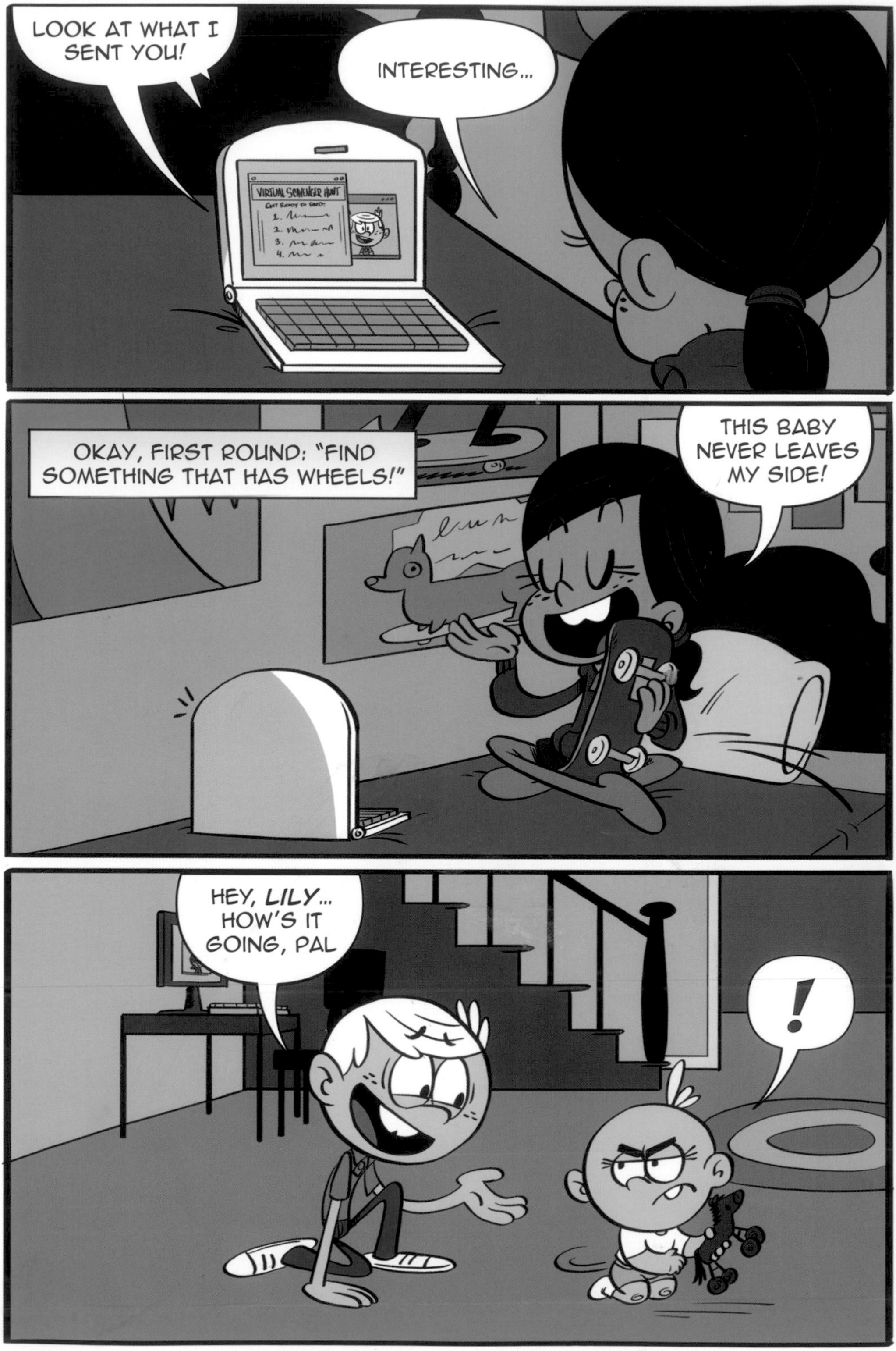
LOOK AT WHAT I SENT YOU!
INTERESTING...
VIRTUAL SCAVENGER HUNT
OKAY, FIRST ROUND: "FIND SOMETHING THAT HAS WHEELS!"
THIS BABY NEVER LEAVES MY SIDE!
HEY, LILY... HOW'S IT GOING, PAL
!

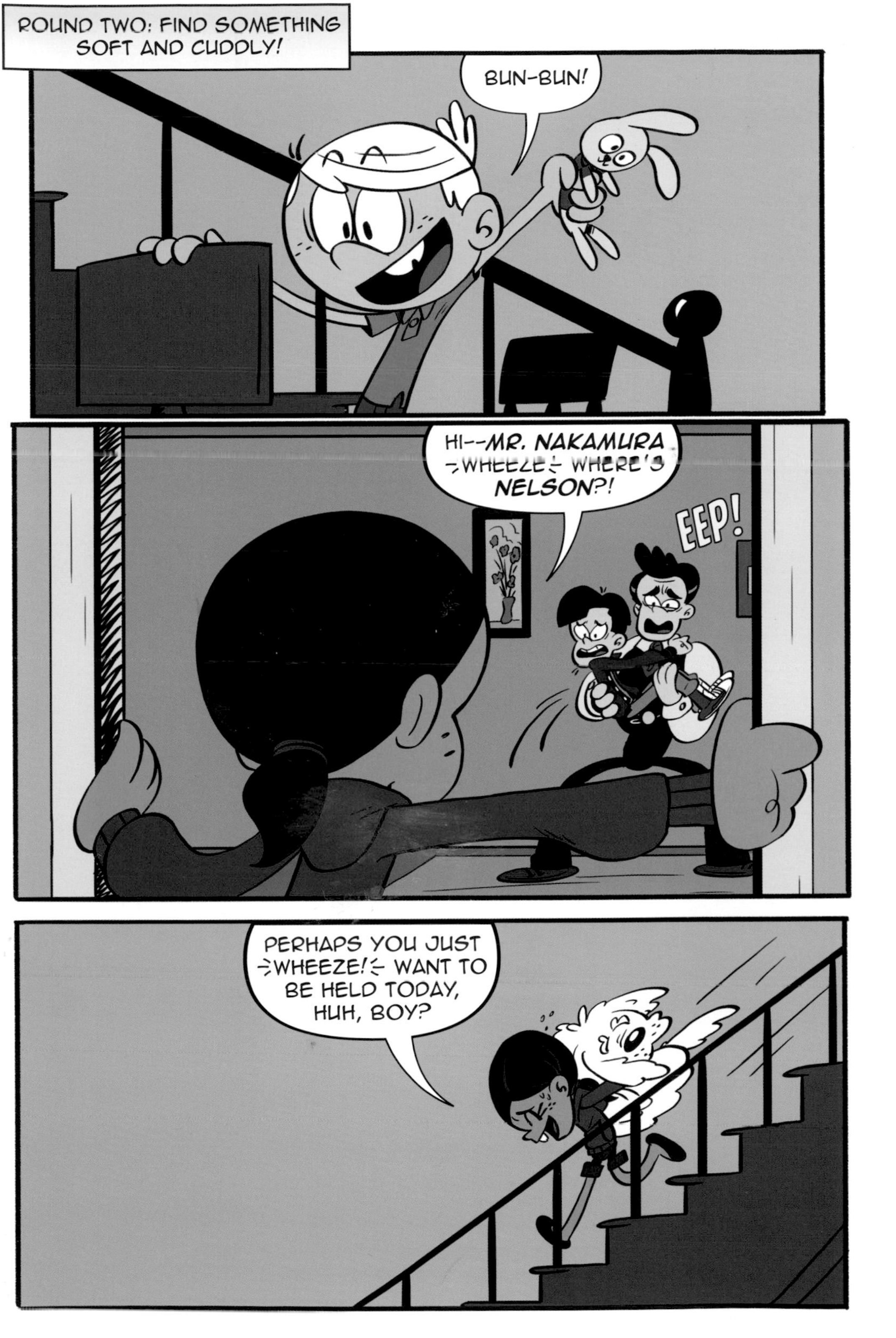
ROUND TWO: FIND SOMETHING SOFT AND CUDDLY!
BUN-BUN!
HI--MR. NAKAMURA -WHEEZE!- WHERE'S NELSON?!
EEP!
PERHAPS YOU JUST -WHEEZE!- WANT TO BE HELD TODAY, HUH, BOY?

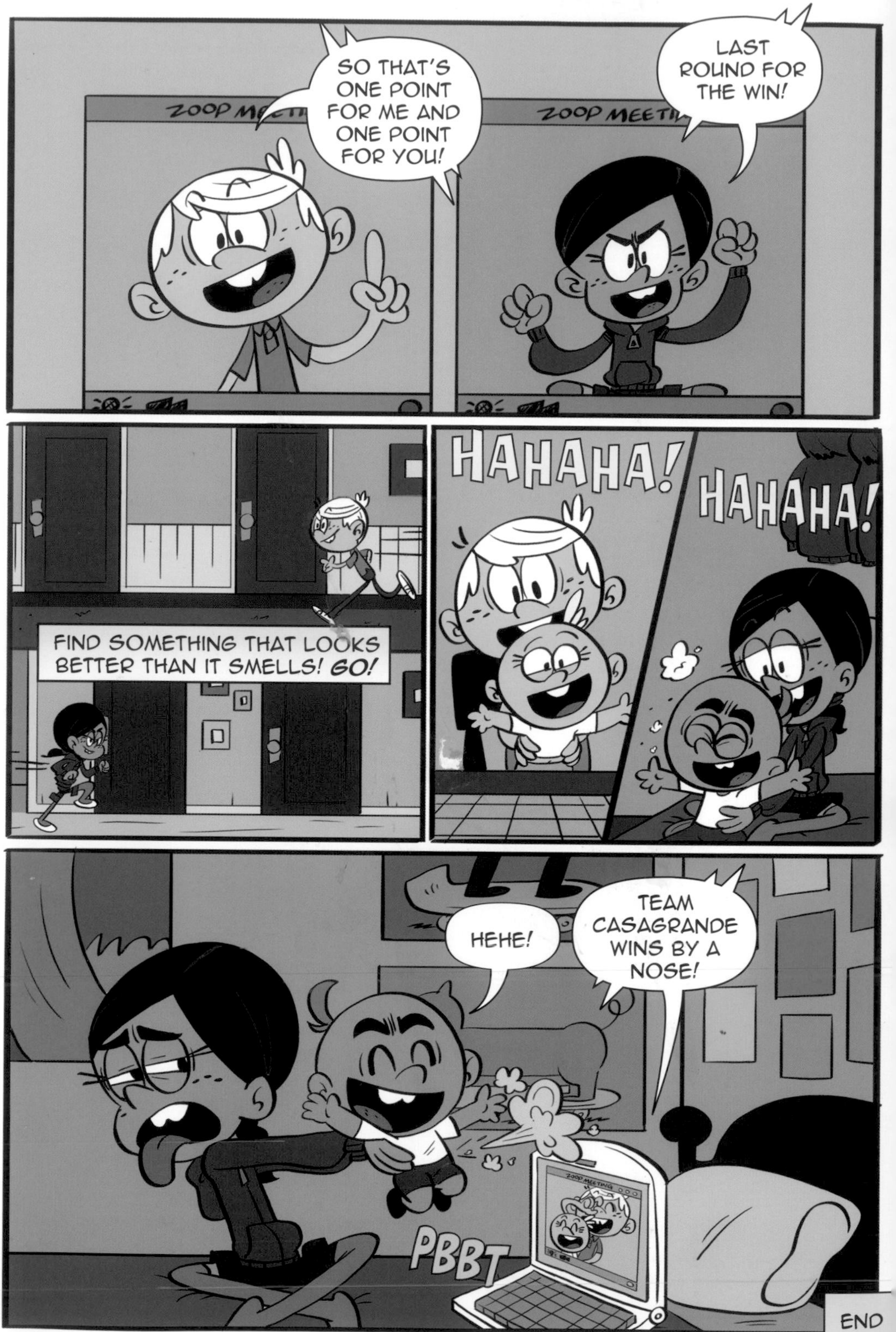
ZOOP MEETI
SO THAT'S ONE POINT FOR ME AND ONE POINT FOR YOU!
ZOOP MEETI
LAST ROUND FOR THE WIN!
FIND SOMETHING THAT LOOKS BETTER THAN IT SMELLS! GO!
HAHAHA!
HAHAHA!
HEHE!
TEAM CASAGRANDE WINS BY A NOSE!
PBBT
ZOOP MEETING
END

"MEOW OR NEVER"

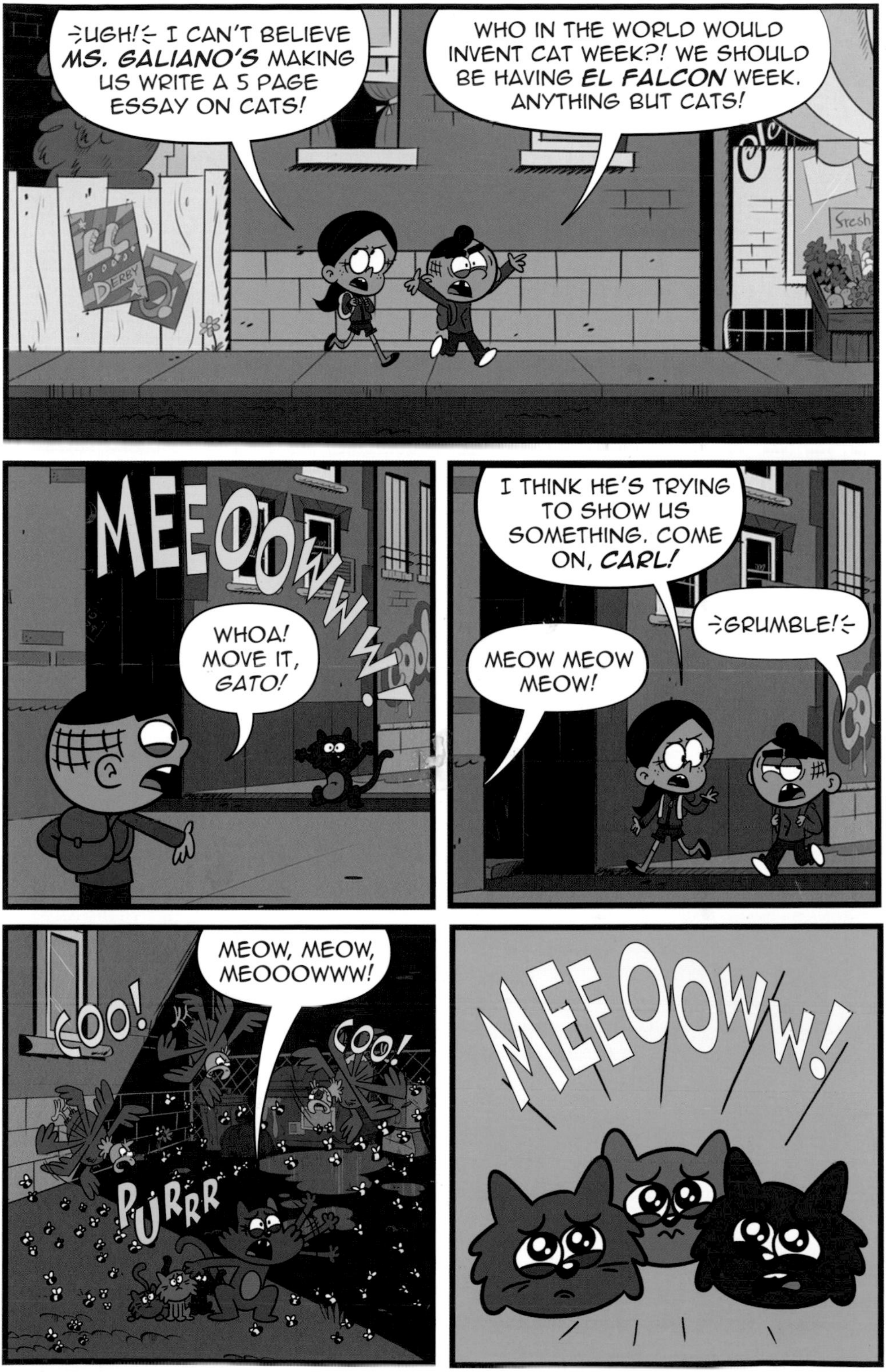

UGH! I CAN'T BELIEVE MS. GALIANO'S MAKING US WRITE A 5 PAGE ESSAY ON CATS!
WHO IN THE WORLD WOULD INVENT CAT WEEK?! WE SHOULD BE HAVING EL FALCON WEEK. ANYTHING BUT CATS!
DERBY
Fresh
MEEOOWWW!
WHOA! MOVE IT, GATO!
I THINK HE'S TRYING TO SHOW US SOMETHING. COME ON, CARL!
GRUMBLE!
MEOW MEOW MEOW!
MEOW, MEOW, MEOOOWWW!
COO!
COO!
PURRR
MEEOOWW!

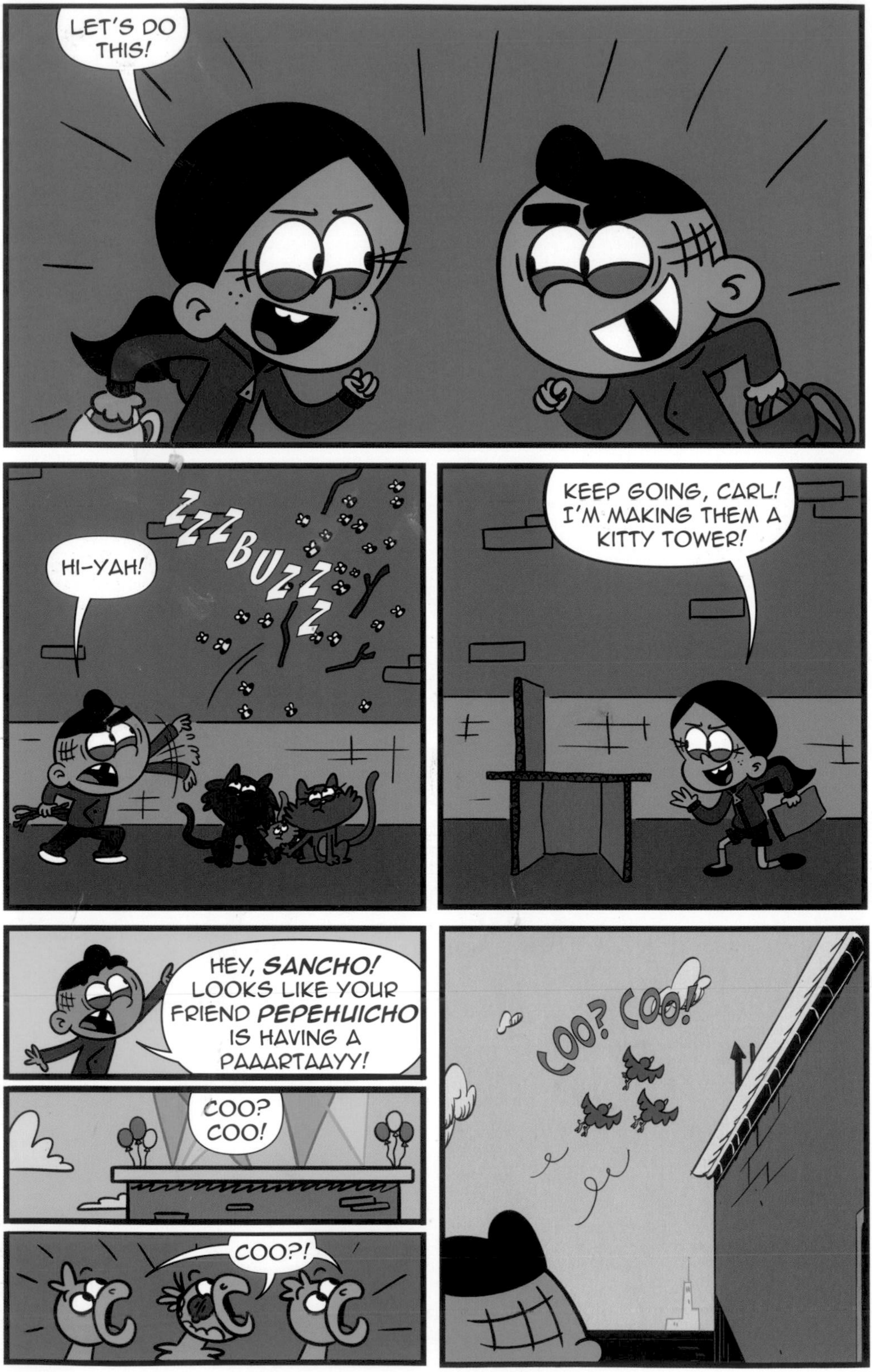
LET'S DO THIS!
ZZZBUZZZZ
HI-YAH!
KEEP GOING, CARL! I'M MAKING THEM A KITTY TOWER!
HEY, *SANCHO!* LOOKS LIKE YOUR FRIEND *PEPEHUICHO* IS HAVING A PAAARTAAYY!
COO? COO!
COO?!
COO? COO!

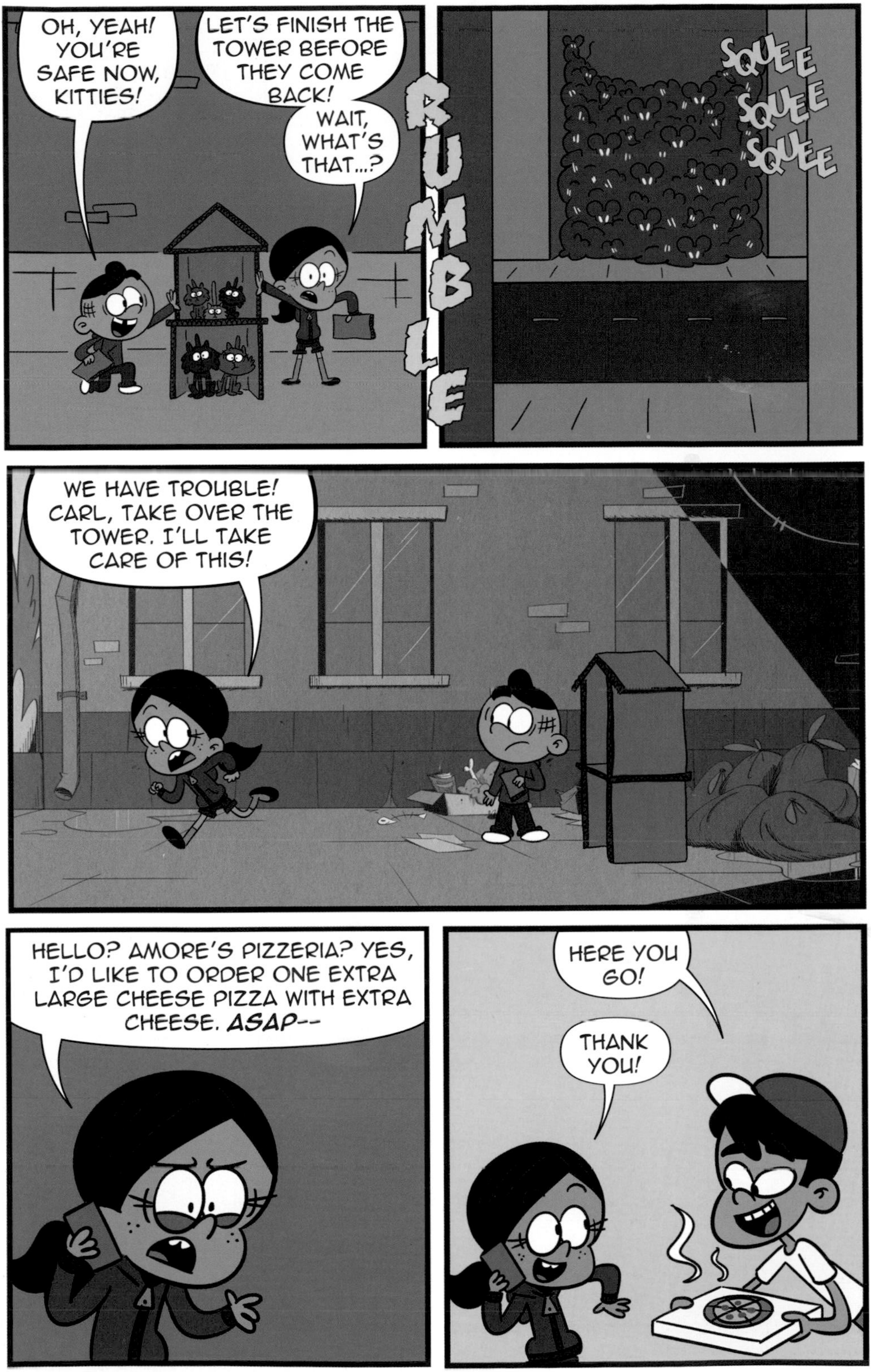
OH, YEAH! YOU'RE SAFE NOW, KITTIES!
LET'S FINISH THE TOWER BEFORE THEY COME BACK!
WAIT, WHAT'S THAT...?
RUMBLE
SQUEEE
SQUEEE
SQUEEE
WE HAVE TROUBLE! CARL, TAKE OVER THE TOWER. I'LL TAKE CARE OF THIS!
HELLO? AMORE'S PIZZERIA? YES, I'D LIKE TO ORDER ONE EXTRA LARGE CHEESE PIZZA WITH EXTRA CHEESE. ASAP--
HERE YOU GO!
THANK YOU!

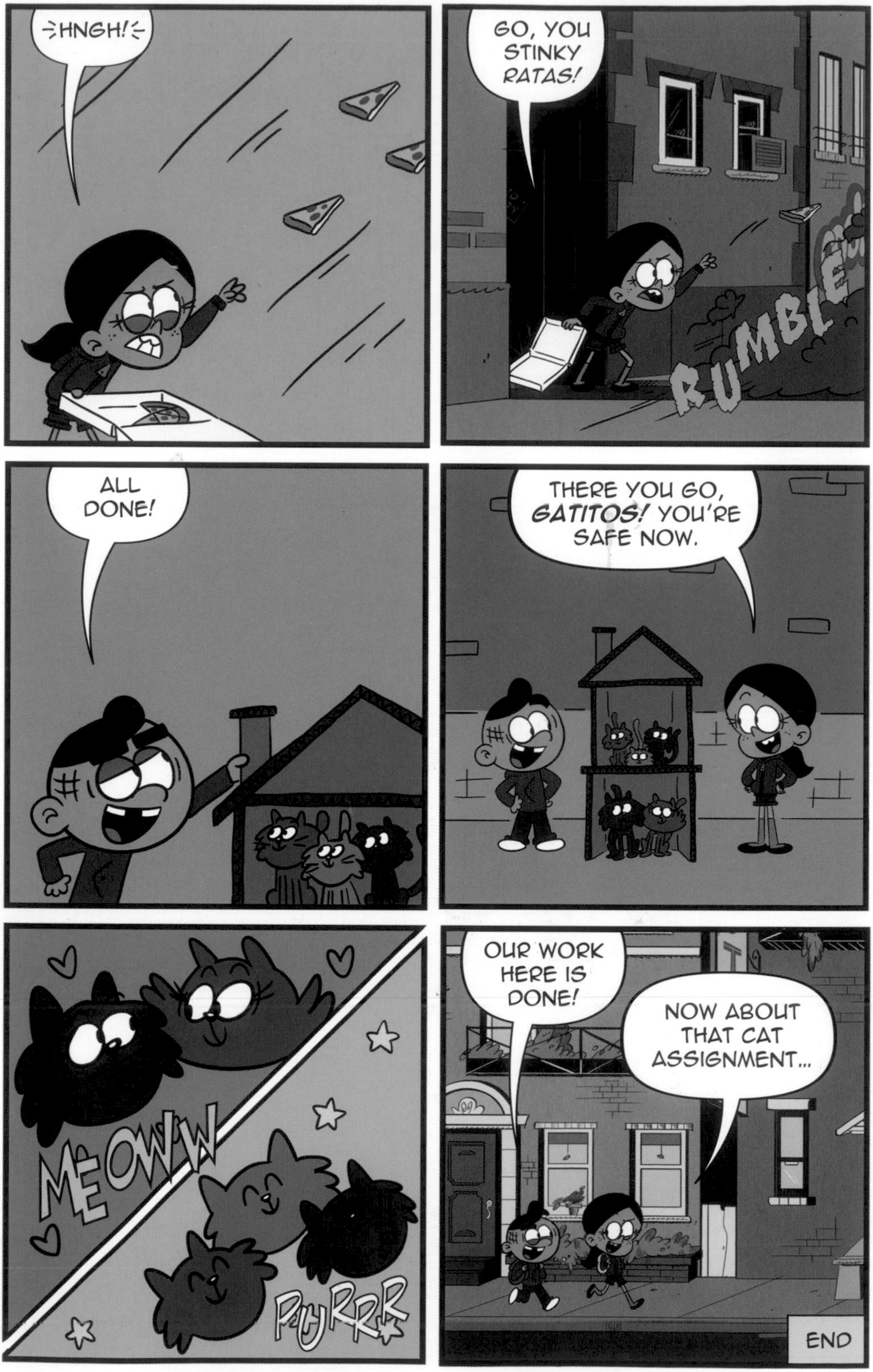
HNGH!
GO, YOU STINKY RATAS!
RUMBLE
ALL DONE!
THERE YOU GO, GATITOS! YOU'RE SAFE NOW.
MEOWW
PURRR
OUR WORK HERE IS DONE!
NOW ABOUT THAT CAT ASSIGNMENT...
END

"THE MEET UP"

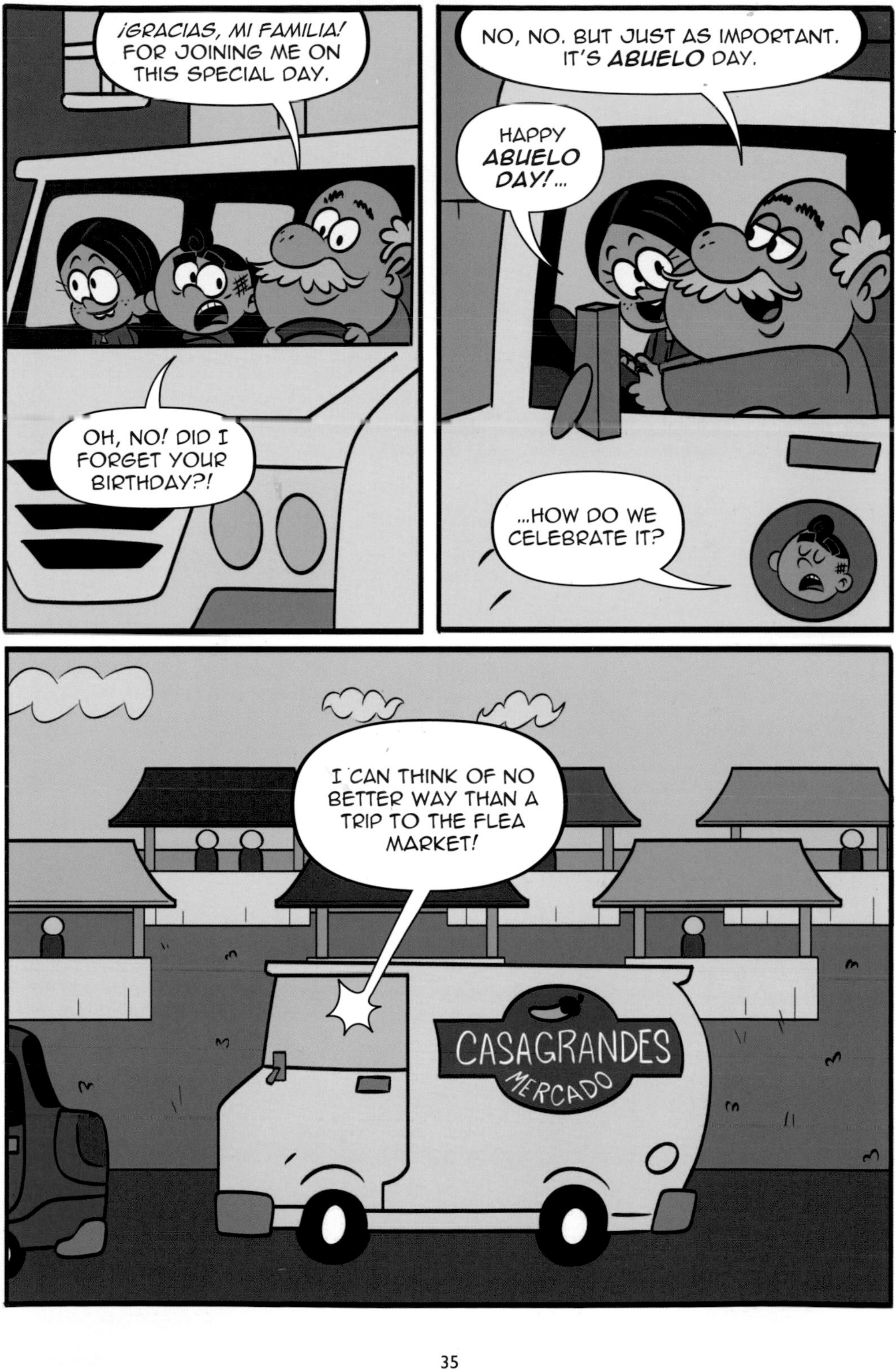
¡GRACIAS, MI FAMILIA! FOR JOINING ME ON THIS SPECIAL DAY.
OH, NO! DID I FORGET YOUR BIRTHDAY?!
NO, NO. BUT JUST AS IMPORTANT. IT'S ABUELO DAY.
HAPPY ABUELO DAY! ...
...HOW DO WE CELEBRATE IT?
I CAN THINK OF NO BETTER WAY THAN A TRIP TO THE FLEA MARKET!
CASAGRANDES MERCADO

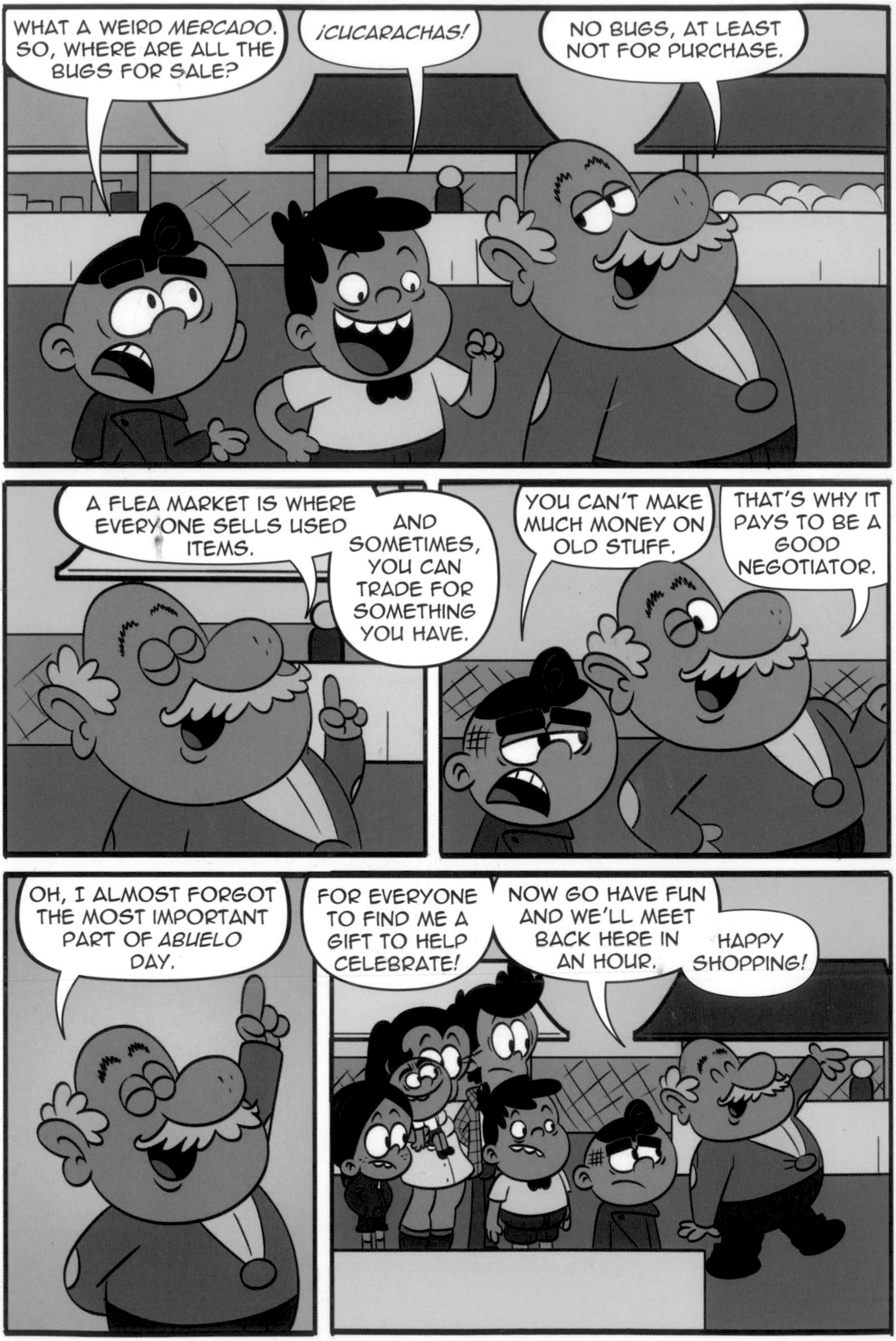
WHAT A WEIRD *MERCADO*. SO, WHERE ARE ALL THE BUGS FOR SALE?
¡CUCARACHAS!
NO BUGS, AT LEAST NOT FOR PURCHASE.
A FLEA MARKET IS WHERE EVERYONE SELLS USED ITEMS.
AND SOMETIMES, YOU CAN TRADE FOR SOMETHING YOU HAVE.
YOU CAN'T MAKE MUCH MONEY ON OLD STUFF.
THAT'S WHY IT PAYS TO BE A GOOD NEGOTIATOR.
OH, I ALMOST FORGOT THE MOST IMPORTANT PART OF *ABUELO* DAY.
FOR EVERYONE TO FIND ME A GIFT TO HELP CELEBRATE!
NOW GO HAVE FUN AND WE'LL MEET BACK HERE IN AN HOUR.
HAPPY SHOPPING!

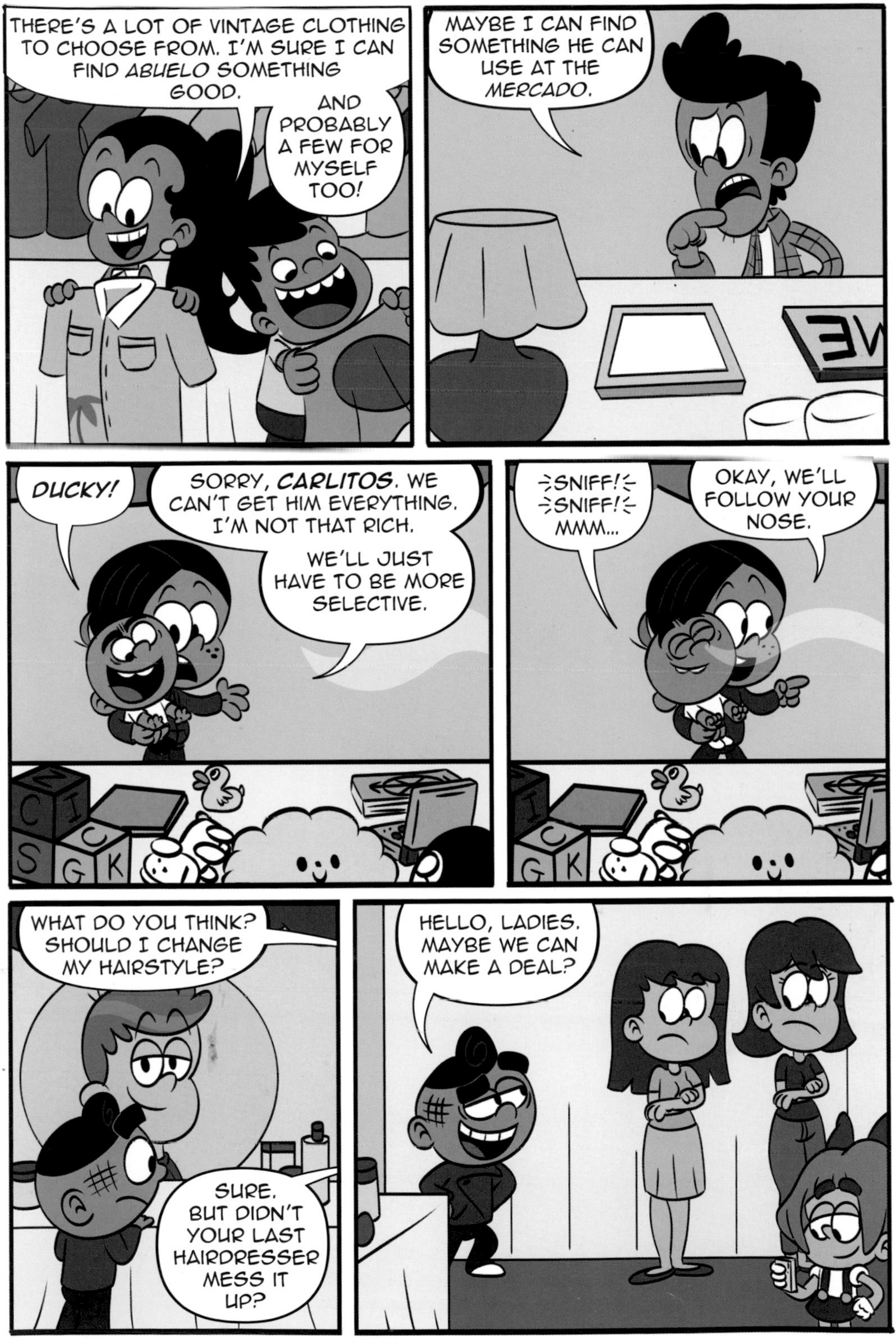
THERE'S A LOT OF VINTAGE CLOTHING TO CHOOSE FROM. I'M SURE I CAN FIND *ABUELO* SOMETHING GOOD.
AND PROBABLY A FEW FOR MYSELF TOO!
MAYBE I CAN FIND SOMETHING HE CAN USE AT THE *MERCADO*.
DUCKY!
SORRY, **CARLITOS**. WE CAN'T GET HIM EVERYTHING. I'M NOT THAT RICH.
WE'LL JUST HAVE TO BE MORE SELECTIVE.
SNIFF! SNIFF! MMM...
OKAY, WE'LL FOLLOW YOUR NOSE.
WHAT DO YOU THINK? SHOULD I CHANGE MY HAIRSTYLE?
SURE. BUT DIDN'T YOUR LAST HAIRDRESSER MESS IT UP?
HELLO, LADIES. MAYBE WE CAN MAKE A DEAL?

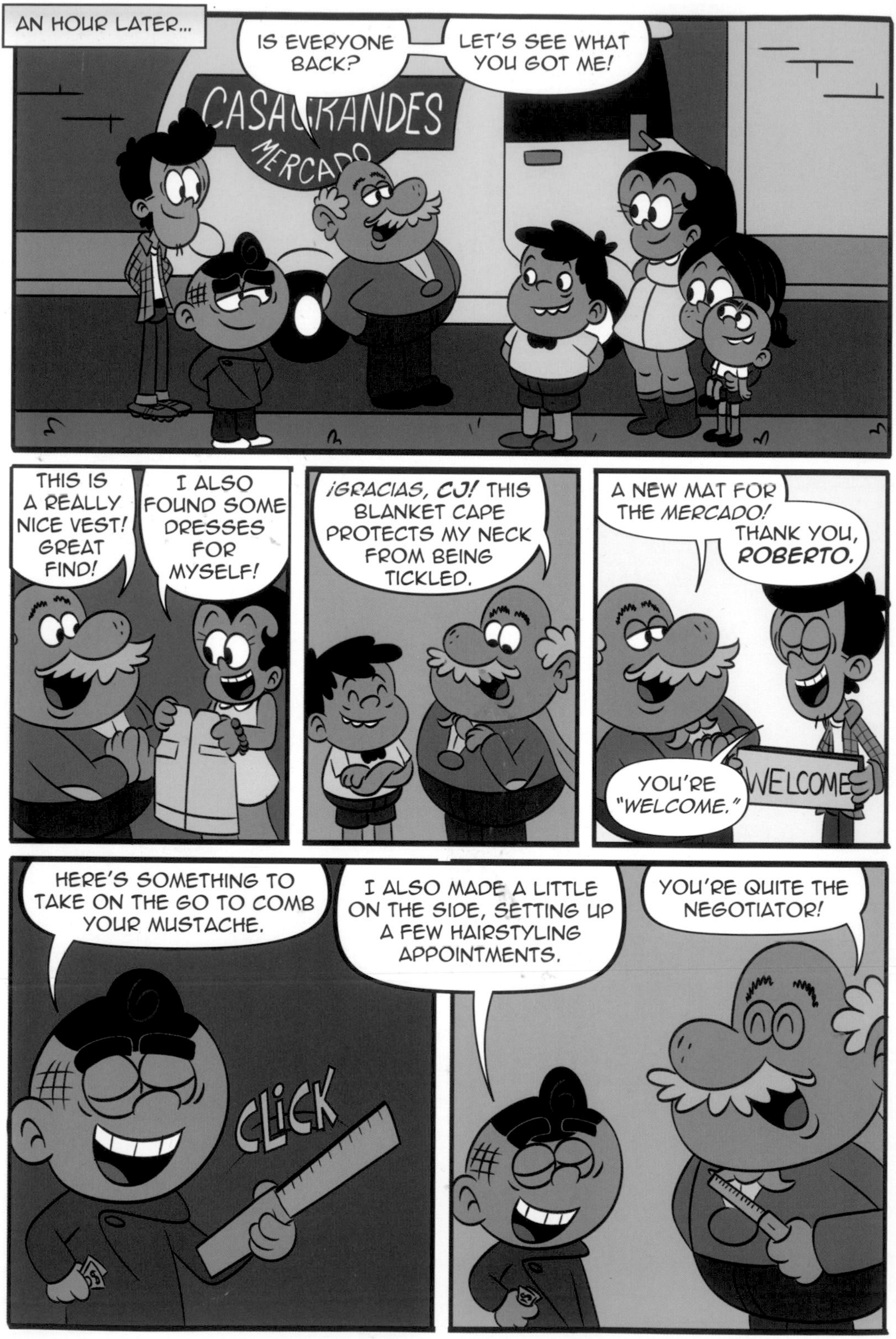
AN HOUR LATER...
IS EVERYONE BACK?
LET'S SEE WHAT YOU GOT ME!
CASAGRANDES MERCADO
THIS IS A REALLY NICE VEST! GREAT FIND!
I ALSO FOUND SOME DRESSES FOR MYSELF!
¡GRACIAS, CJ! THIS BLANKET CAPE PROTECTS MY NECK FROM BEING TICKLED.
A NEW MAT FOR THE MERCADO! THANK YOU, ROBERTO.
YOU'RE "WELCOME."
WELCOME
HERE'S SOMETHING TO TAKE ON THE GO TO COMB YOUR MUSTACHE.
CLICK
I ALSO MADE A LITTLE ON THE SIDE, SETTING UP A FEW HAIRSTYLING APPOINTMENTS.
YOU'RE QUITE THE NEGOTIATOR!

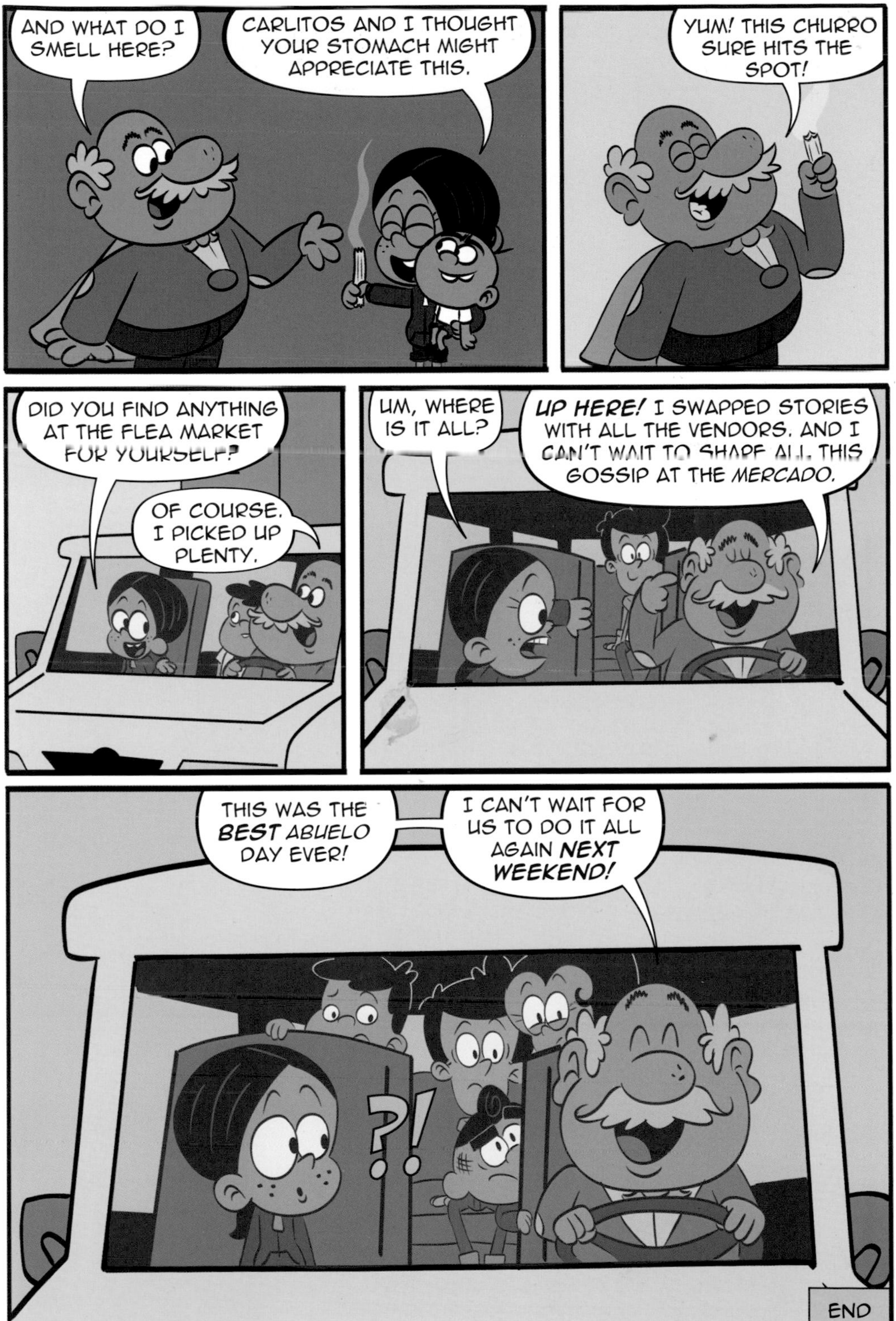
AND WHAT DO I SMELL HERE?
CARLITOS AND I THOUGHT YOUR STOMACH MIGHT APPRECIATE THIS.
YUM! THIS CHURRO SURE HITS THE SPOT!
DID YOU FIND ANYTHING AT THE FLEA MARKET FOR YOURSELF?
OF COURSE. I PICKED UP PLENTY.
UM, WHERE IS IT ALL?
UP HERE! I SWAPPED STORIES WITH ALL THE VENDORS. AND I CAN'T WAIT TO SHARE ALL THIS GOSSIP AT THE MERCADO.
THIS WAS THE BEST ABUELO DAY EVER!
I CAN'T WAIT FOR US TO DO IT ALL AGAIN NEXT WEEKEND!
?!
END

"SELL BY LATE"

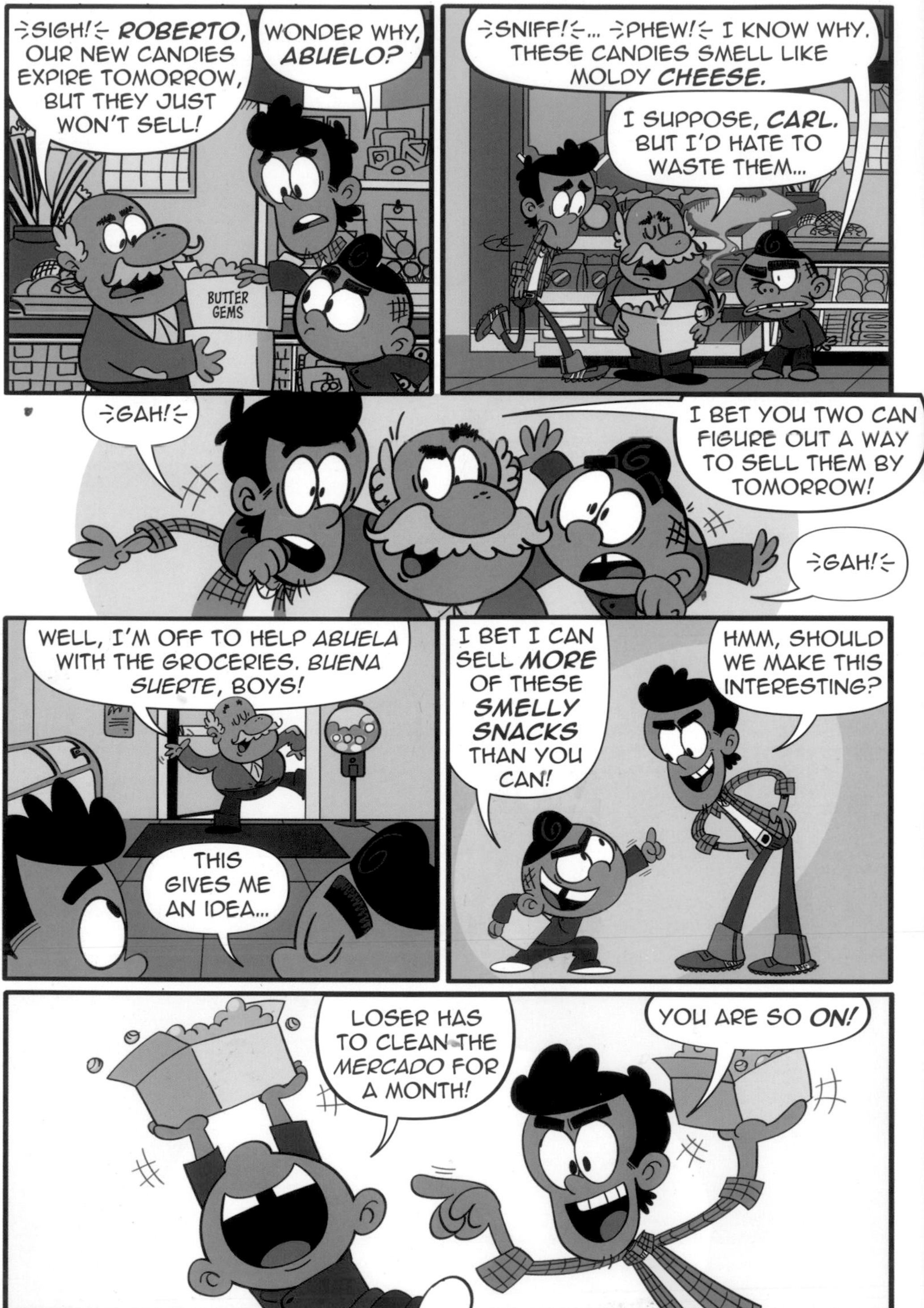

SIGH! ROBERTO, OUR NEW CANDIES EXPIRE TOMORROW, BUT THEY JUST WON'T SELL!
WONDER WHY, ABUELO?
BUTTER GEMS
SNIFF!... PHEW! I KNOW WHY. THESE CANDIES SMELL LIKE MOLDY CHEESE.
I SUPPOSE, CARL. BUT I'D HATE TO WASTE THEM...
GAH!
I BET YOU TWO CAN FIGURE OUT A WAY TO SELL THEM BY TOMORROW!
GAH!
WELL, I'M OFF TO HELP ABUELA WITH THE GROCERIES. BUENA SUERTE, BOYS!
THIS GIVES ME AN IDEA...
I BET I CAN SELL MORE OF THESE SMELLY SNACKS THAN YOU CAN!
HMM, SHOULD WE MAKE THIS INTERESTING?
LOSER HAS TO CLEAN THE MERCADO FOR A MONTH!
YOU ARE SO ON!

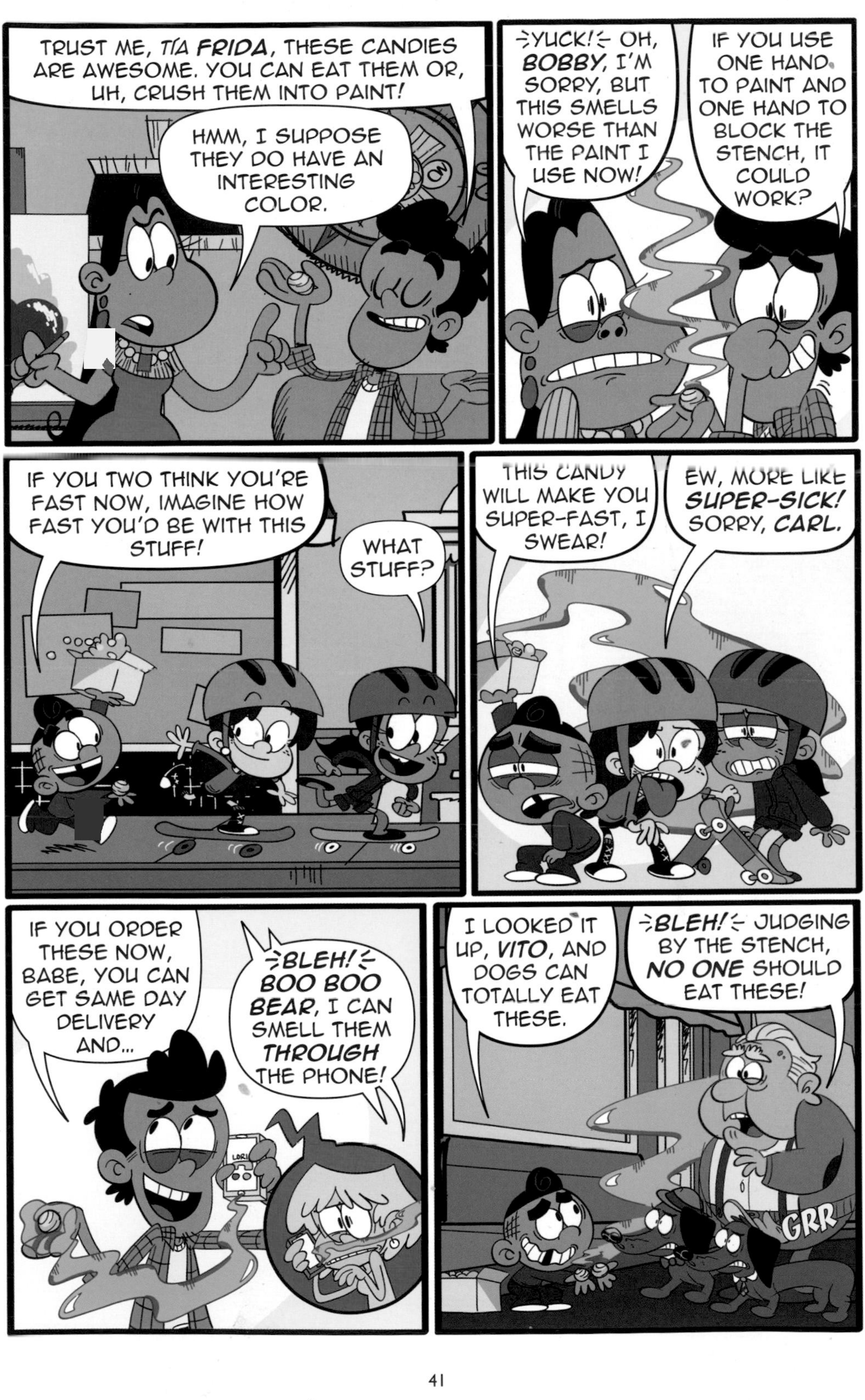

TRUST ME, TÍA FRIDA, THESE CANDIES ARE AWESOME. YOU CAN EAT THEM OR, UH, CRUSH THEM INTO PAINT!
HMM, I SUPPOSE THEY DO HAVE AN INTERESTING COLOR.
YUCK! OH, BOBBY, I'M SORRY, BUT THIS SMELLS WORSE THAN THE PAINT I USE NOW!
IF YOU USE ONE HAND TO PAINT AND ONE HAND TO BLOCK THE STENCH, IT COULD WORK?
IF YOU TWO THINK YOU'RE FAST NOW, IMAGINE HOW FAST YOU'D BE WITH THIS STUFF!
WHAT STUFF?
THIS CANDY WILL MAKE YOU SUPER-FAST, I SWEAR!
EW, MORE LIKE SUPER-SICK! SORRY, CARL.
IF YOU ORDER THESE NOW, BABE, YOU CAN GET SAME DAY DELIVERY AND...
BLEH! BOO BOO BEAR, I CAN SMELL THEM THROUGH THE PHONE!
LORI
I LOOKED IT UP, VITO, AND DOGS CAN TOTALLY EAT THESE.
BLEH! JUDGING BY THE STENCH, NO ONE SHOULD EAT THESE!
GRR

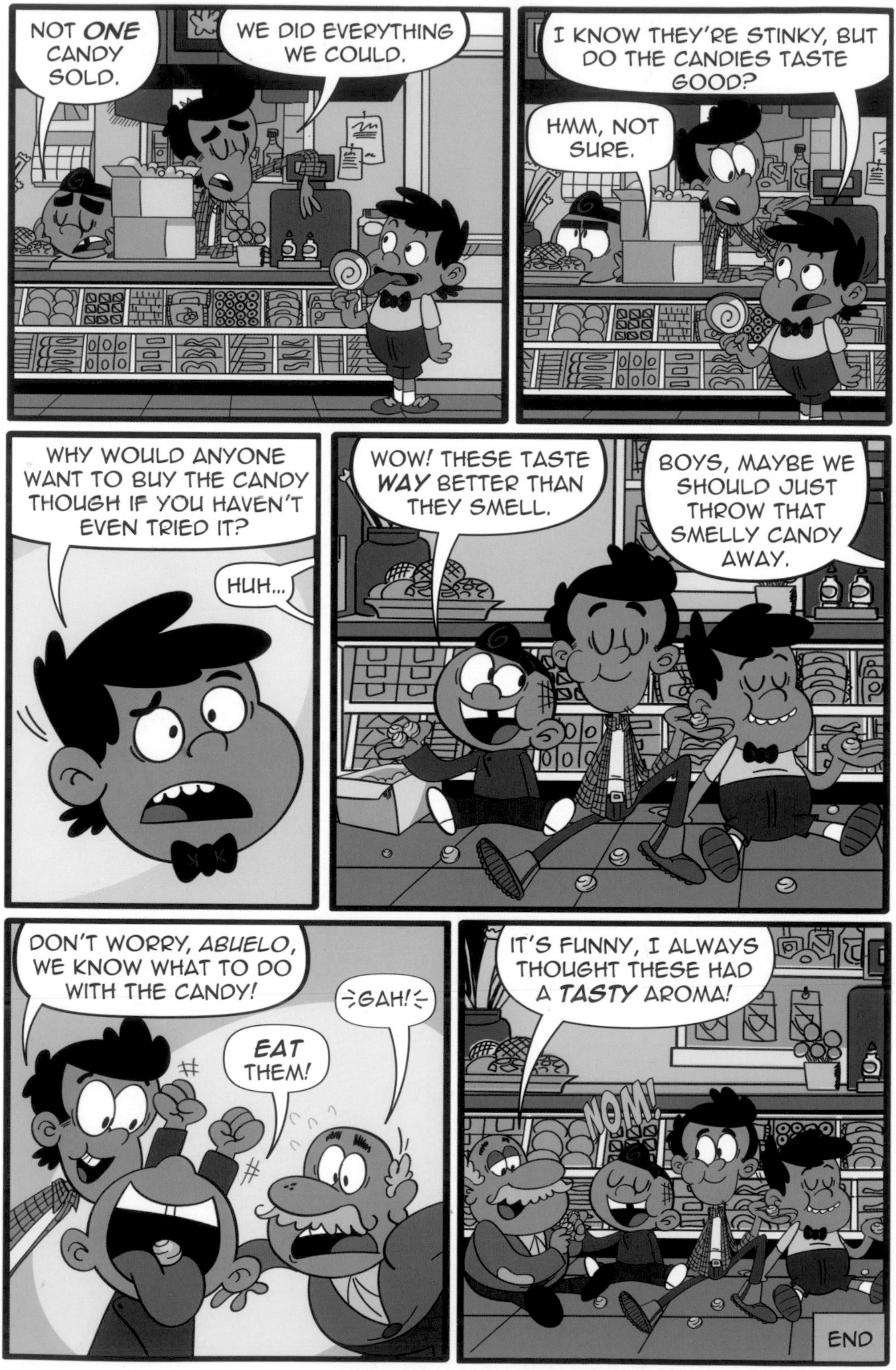
NOT ONE CANDY SOLD.
WE DID EVERYTHING WE COULD.
I KNOW THEY'RE STINKY, BUT DO THE CANDIES TASTE GOOD?
HMM, NOT SURE.
WHY WOULD ANYONE WANT TO BUY THE CANDY THOUGH IF YOU HAVEN'T EVEN TRIED IT?
HUH...
WOW! THESE TASTE WAY BETTER THAN THEY SMELL.
BOYS, MAYBE WE SHOULD JUST THROW THAT SMELLY CANDY AWAY.
DON'T WORRY, ABUELO, WE KNOW WHAT TO DO WITH THE CANDY!
GAH!
EAT THEM!
IT'S FUNNY, I ALWAYS THOUGHT THESE HAD A TASTY AROMA!
NOM!
END

"THAT'S THE SPIRIT"

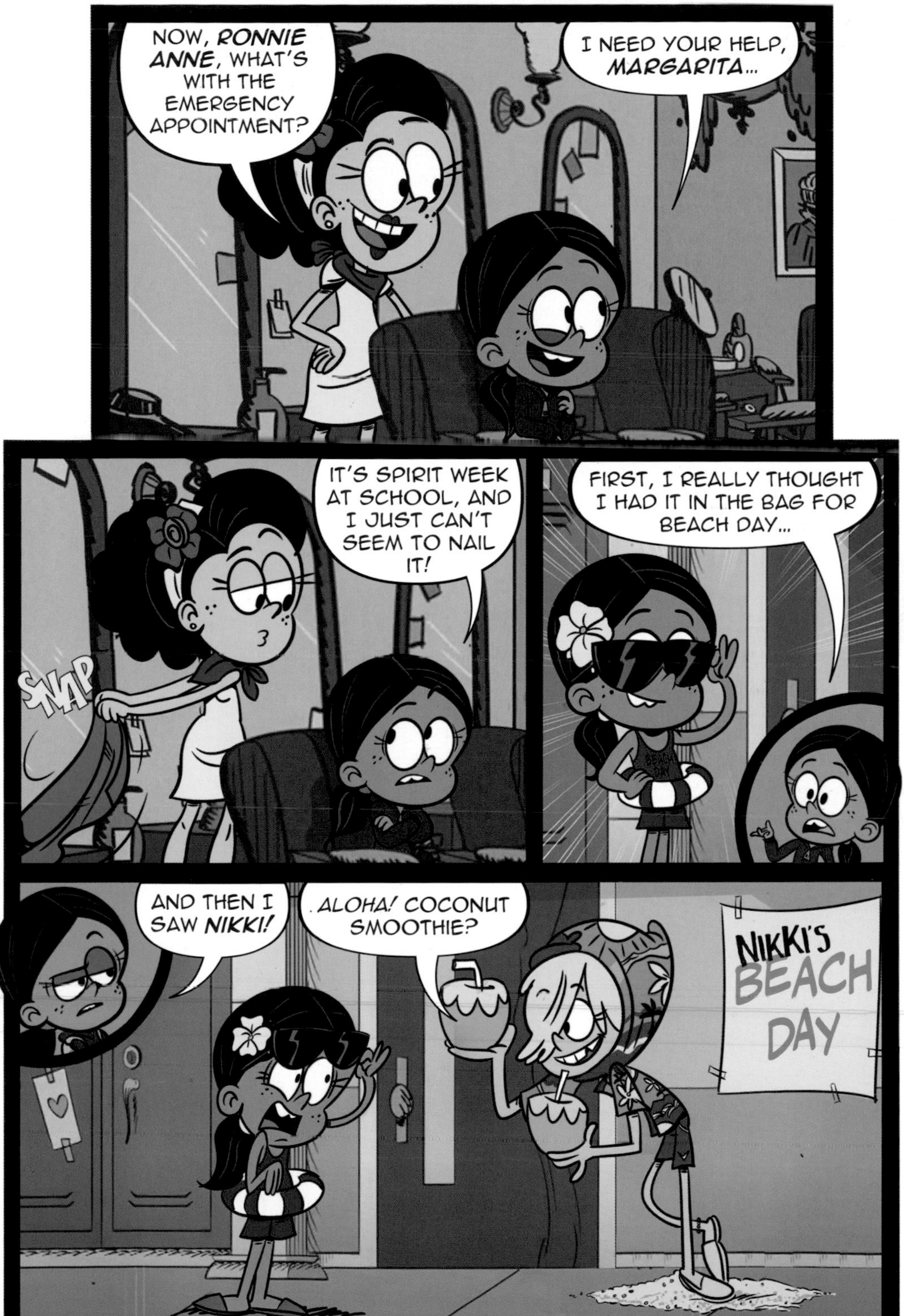
NOW, RONNIE ANNE, WHAT'S WITH THE EMERGENCY APPOINTMENT?
I NEED YOUR HELP, MARGARITA...
SNAP
IT'S SPIRIT WEEK AT SCHOOL, AND I JUST CAN'T SEEM TO NAIL IT!
FIRST, I REALLY THOUGHT I HAD IT IN THE BAG FOR BEACH DAY...
BEACH DAY
AND THEN I SAW NIKKI!
ALOHA! COCONUT SMOOTHIE?
NIKKI'S BEACH DAY

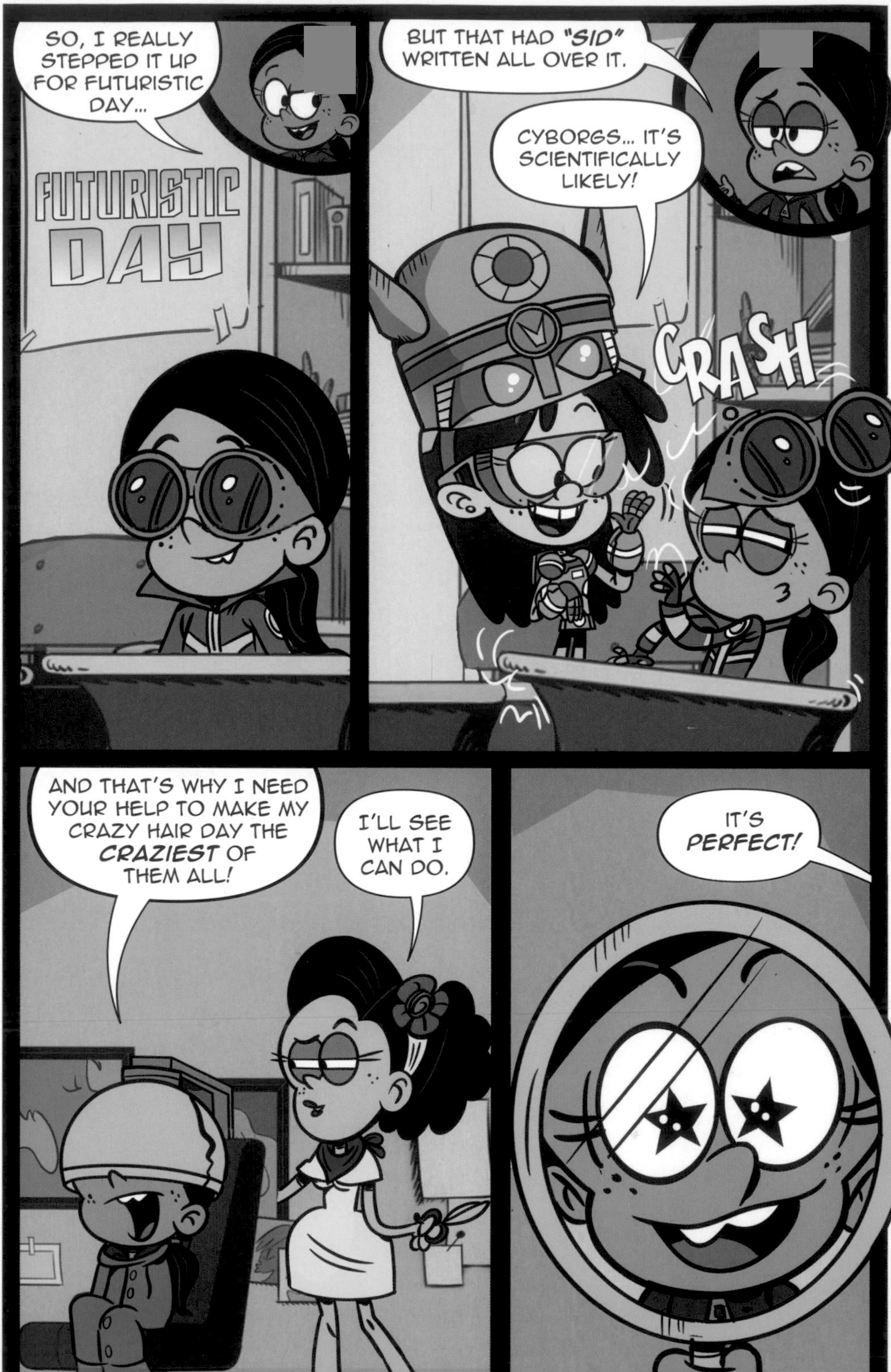
SO, I REALLY STEPPED IT UP FOR FUTURISTIC DAY...
FUTURISTIC DAY
BUT THAT HAD "SID" WRITTEN ALL OVER IT.
CYBORGS... IT'S SCIENTIFICALLY LIKELY!
CRASH
AND THAT'S WHY I NEED YOUR HELP TO MAKE MY CRAZY HAIR DAY THE CRAZIEST OF THEM ALL!
I'LL SEE WHAT I CAN DO.
IT'S PERFECT!

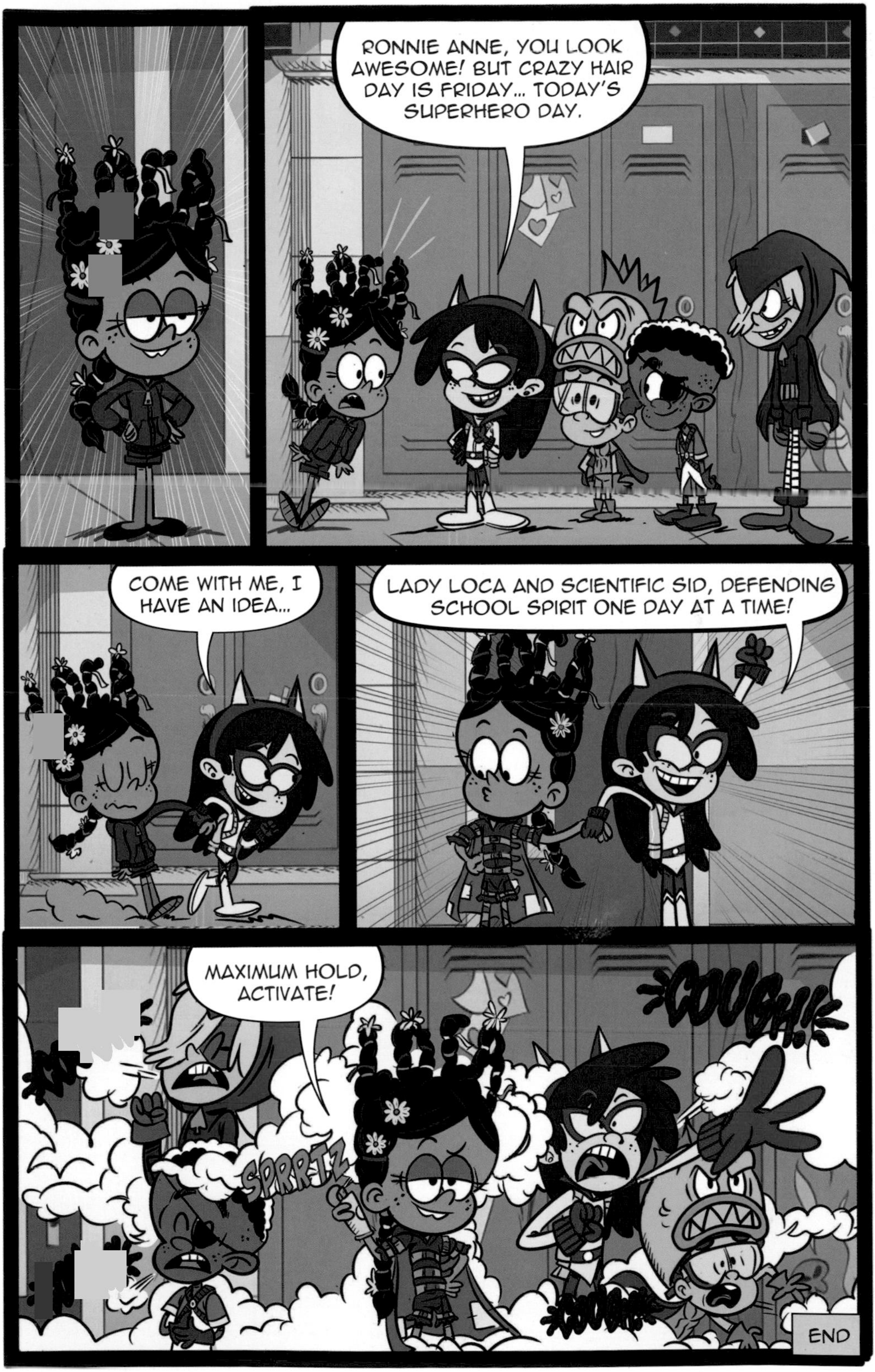
RONNIE ANNE, YOU LOOK AWESOME! BUT CRAZY HAIR DAY IS FRIDAY... TODAY'S SUPERHERO DAY.
COME WITH ME, I HAVE AN IDEA...
LADY LOCA AND SCIENTIFIC SID, DEFENDING SCHOOL SPIRIT ONE DAY AT A TIME!
MAXIMUM HOLD, ACTIVATE!
COUGH!
SPRRTZ
COUGH!
END

"MEATBALL MANIA"

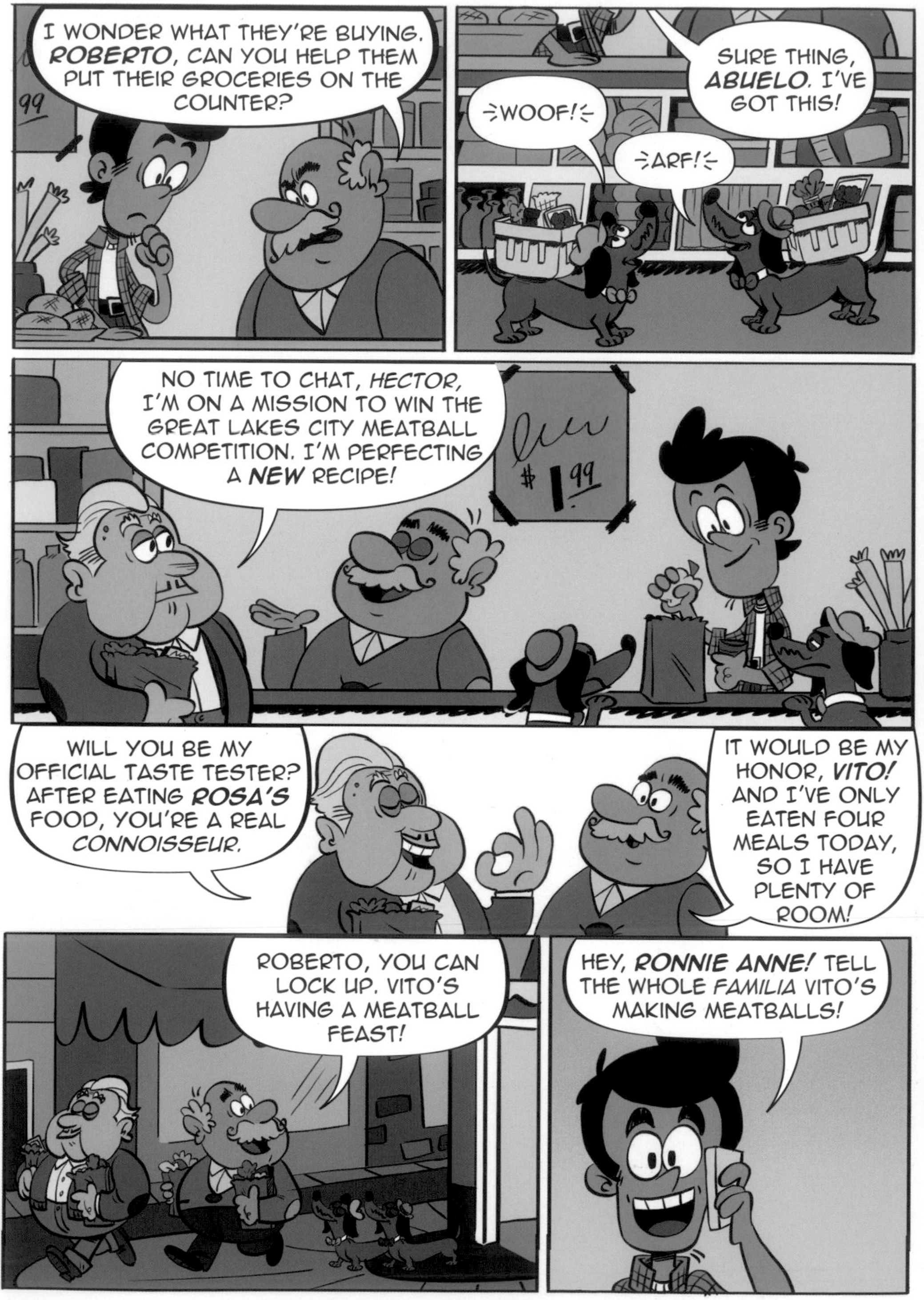
I WONDER WHAT THEY'RE BUYING. *ROBERTO*, CAN YOU HELP THEM PUT THEIR GROCERIES ON THE COUNTER?
SURE THING, *ABUELO*. I'VE GOT THIS!
WOOF!
ARF!
NO TIME TO CHAT, *HECTOR*, I'M ON A MISSION TO WIN THE GREAT LAKES CITY MEATBALL COMPETITION. I'M PERFECTING A *NEW* RECIPE!
$1.99
WILL YOU BE MY OFFICIAL TASTE TESTER? AFTER EATING *ROSA'S* FOOD, YOU'RE A REAL *CONNOISSEUR*.
IT WOULD BE MY HONOR, *VITO!* AND I'VE ONLY EATEN FOUR MEALS TODAY, SO I HAVE PLENTY OF ROOM!
ROBERTO, YOU CAN LOCK UP. VITO'S HAVING A MEATBALL FEAST!
HEY, *RONNIE ANNE!* TELL THE WHOLE *FAMILIA* VITO'S MAKING MEATBALLS!

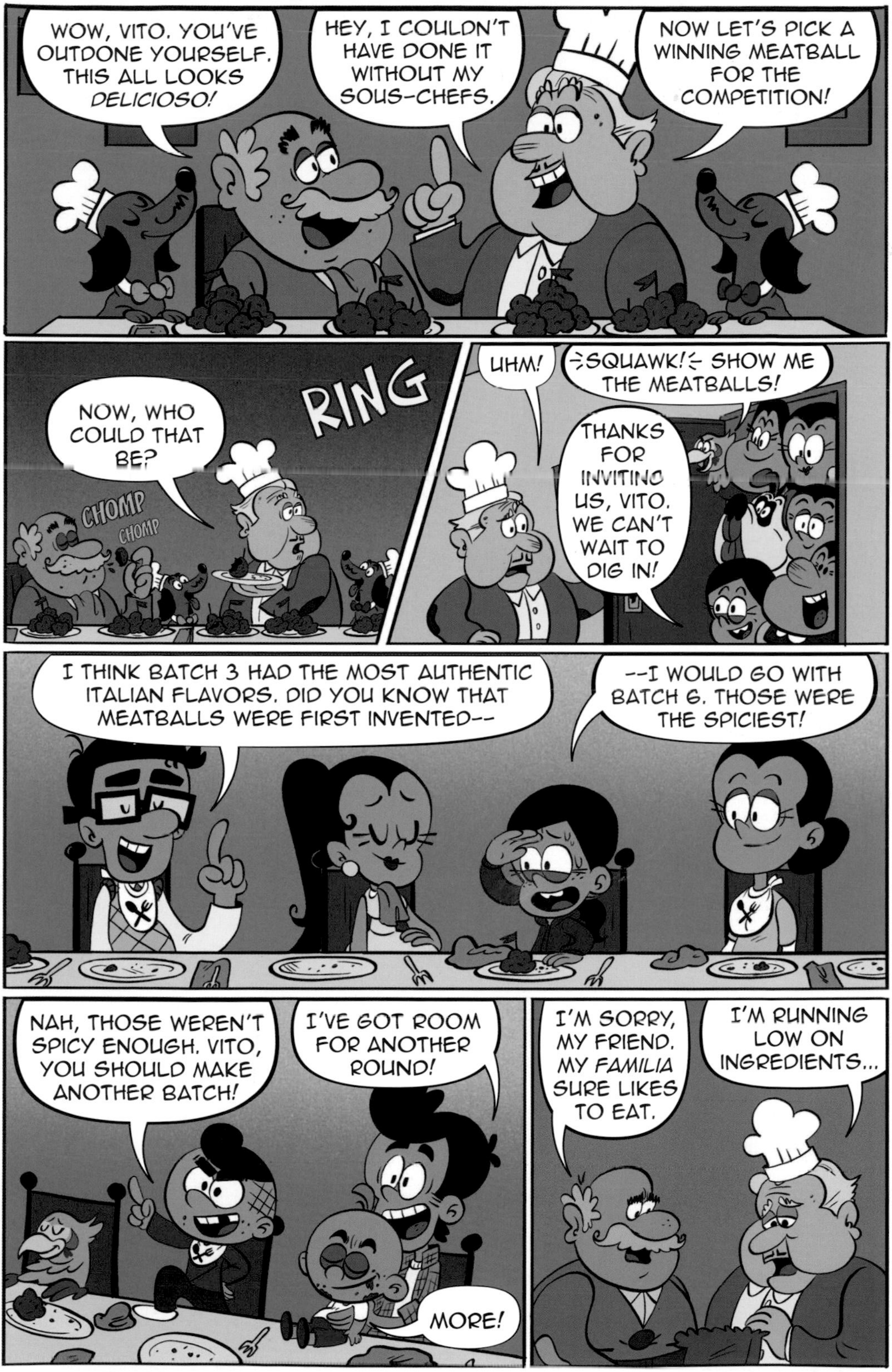
WOW, VITO. YOU'VE OUTDONE YOURSELF. THIS ALL LOOKS *DELICIOSO!*
HEY, I COULDN'T HAVE DONE IT WITHOUT MY SOUS-CHEFS.
NOW LET'S PICK A WINNING MEATBALL FOR THE COMPETITION!
RING
NOW, WHO COULD THAT BE?
CHOMP
CHOMP
UHM!
SQUAWK! SHOW ME THE MEATBALLS!
THANKS FOR INVITING US, VITO. WE CAN'T WAIT TO DIG IN!
I THINK BATCH 3 HAD THE MOST AUTHENTIC ITALIAN FLAVORS. DID YOU KNOW THAT MEATBALLS WERE FIRST INVENTED--
--I WOULD GO WITH BATCH 6. THOSE WERE THE SPICIEST!
NAH, THOSE WEREN'T SPICY ENOUGH. VITO, YOU SHOULD MAKE ANOTHER BATCH!
I'VE GOT ROOM FOR ANOTHER ROUND!
MORE!
I'M SORRY, MY FRIEND. MY *FAMILIA* SURE LIKES TO EAT.
I'M RUNNING LOW ON INGREDIENTS...

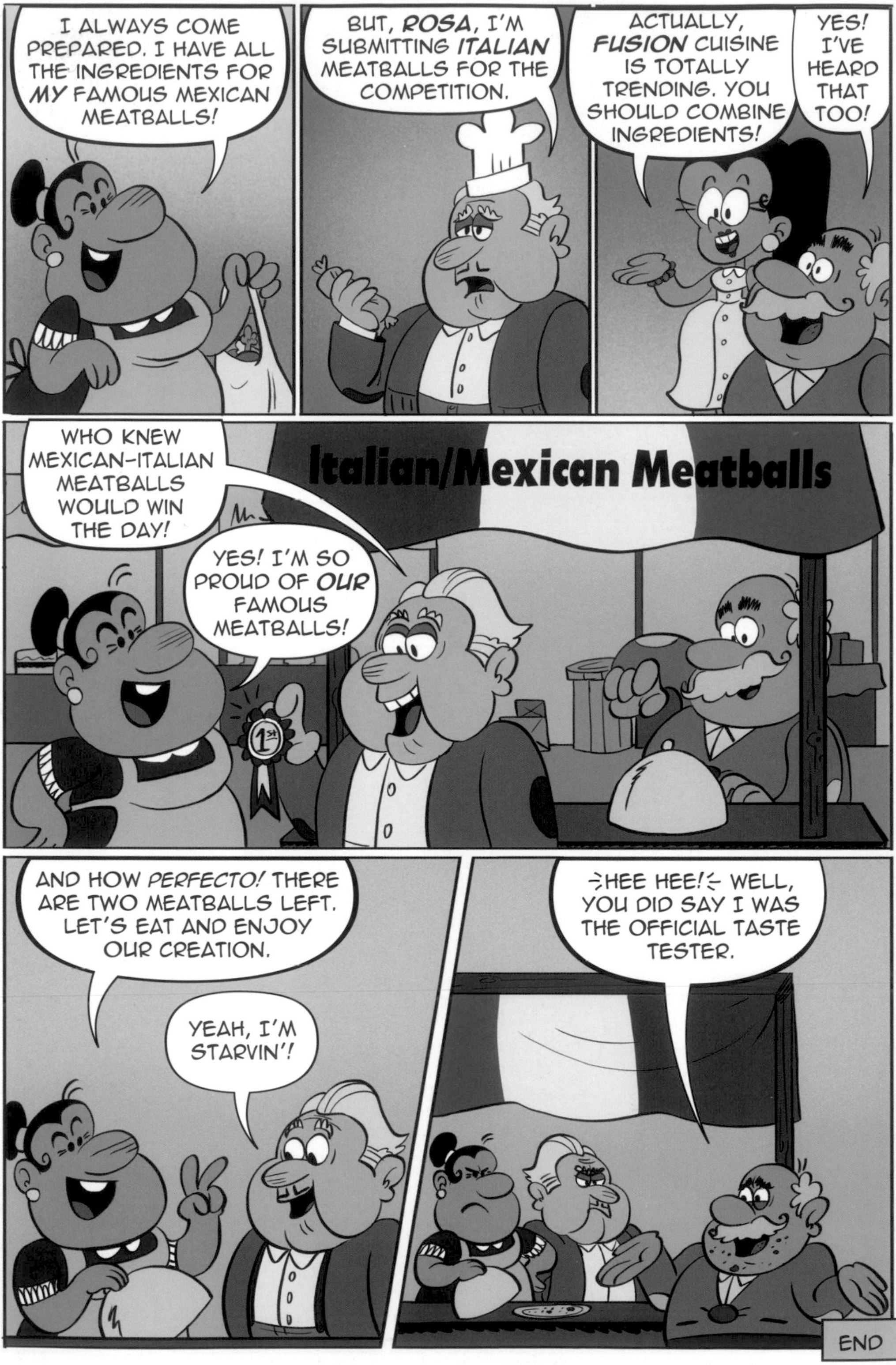
I ALWAYS COME PREPARED. I HAVE ALL THE INGREDIENTS FOR *MY* FAMOUS MEXICAN MEATBALLS!
BUT, *ROSA*, I'M SUBMITTING *ITALIAN* MEATBALLS FOR THE COMPETITION.
ACTUALLY, *FUSION* CUISINE IS TOTALLY TRENDING. YOU SHOULD COMBINE INGREDIENTS!
YES! I'VE HEARD THAT TOO!
Italian/Mexican Meatballs
WHO KNEW MEXICAN-ITALIAN MEATBALLS WOULD WIN THE DAY!
YES! I'M SO PROUD OF *OUR* FAMOUS MEATBALLS!
1st
AND HOW *PERFECTO!* THERE ARE TWO MEATBALLS LEFT. LET'S EAT AND ENJOY OUR CREATION.
YEAH, I'M STARVIN'!
HEE HEE! WELL, YOU DID SAY I WAS THE OFFICIAL TASTE TESTER.
END

"ALL NIGHTER"

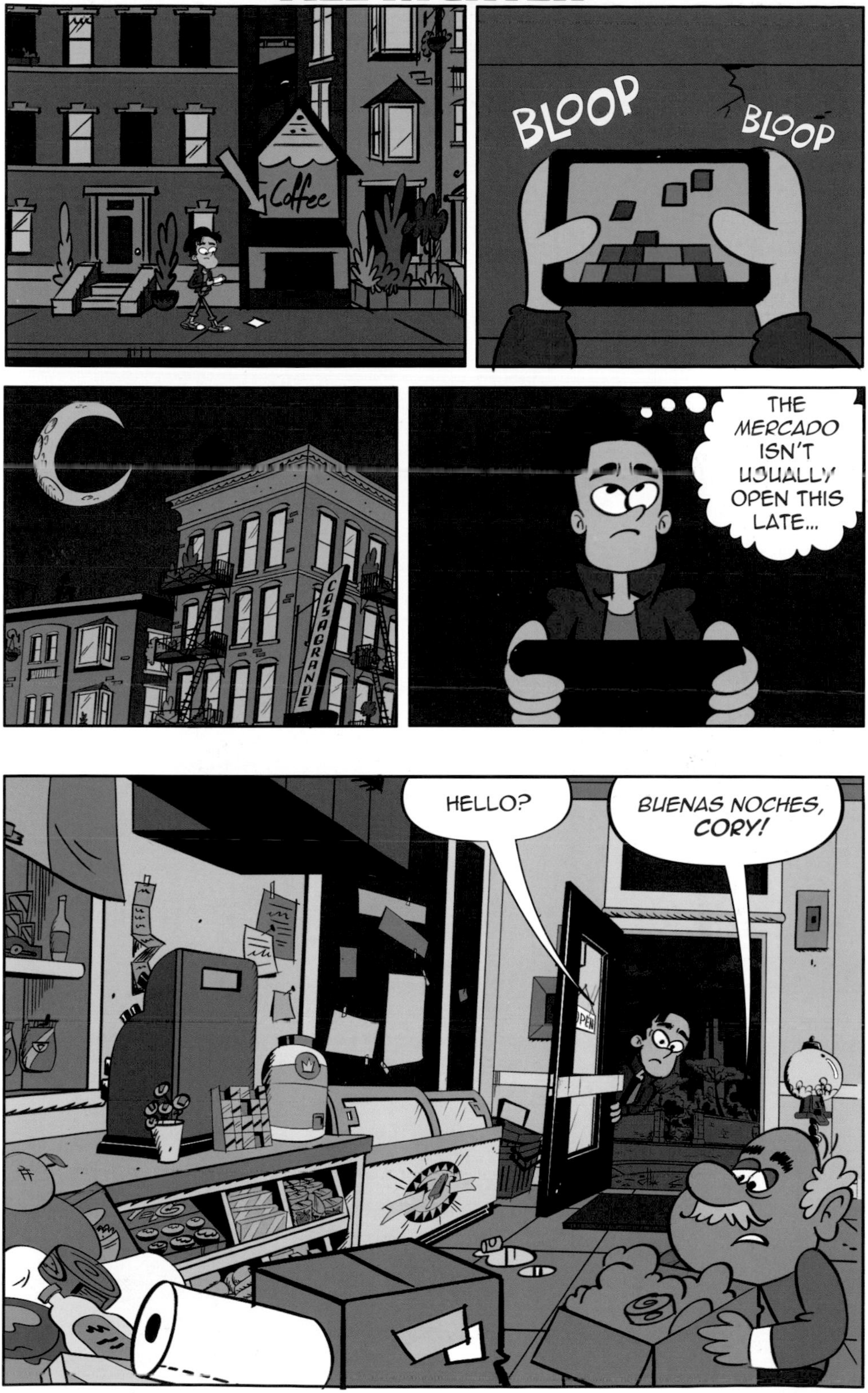
Coffee
BLOOP
BLOOP
THE MERCADO ISN'T USUALLY OPEN THIS LATE...
CASAGRANDE
HELLO?
BUENAS NOCHES, CORY!
OPEN

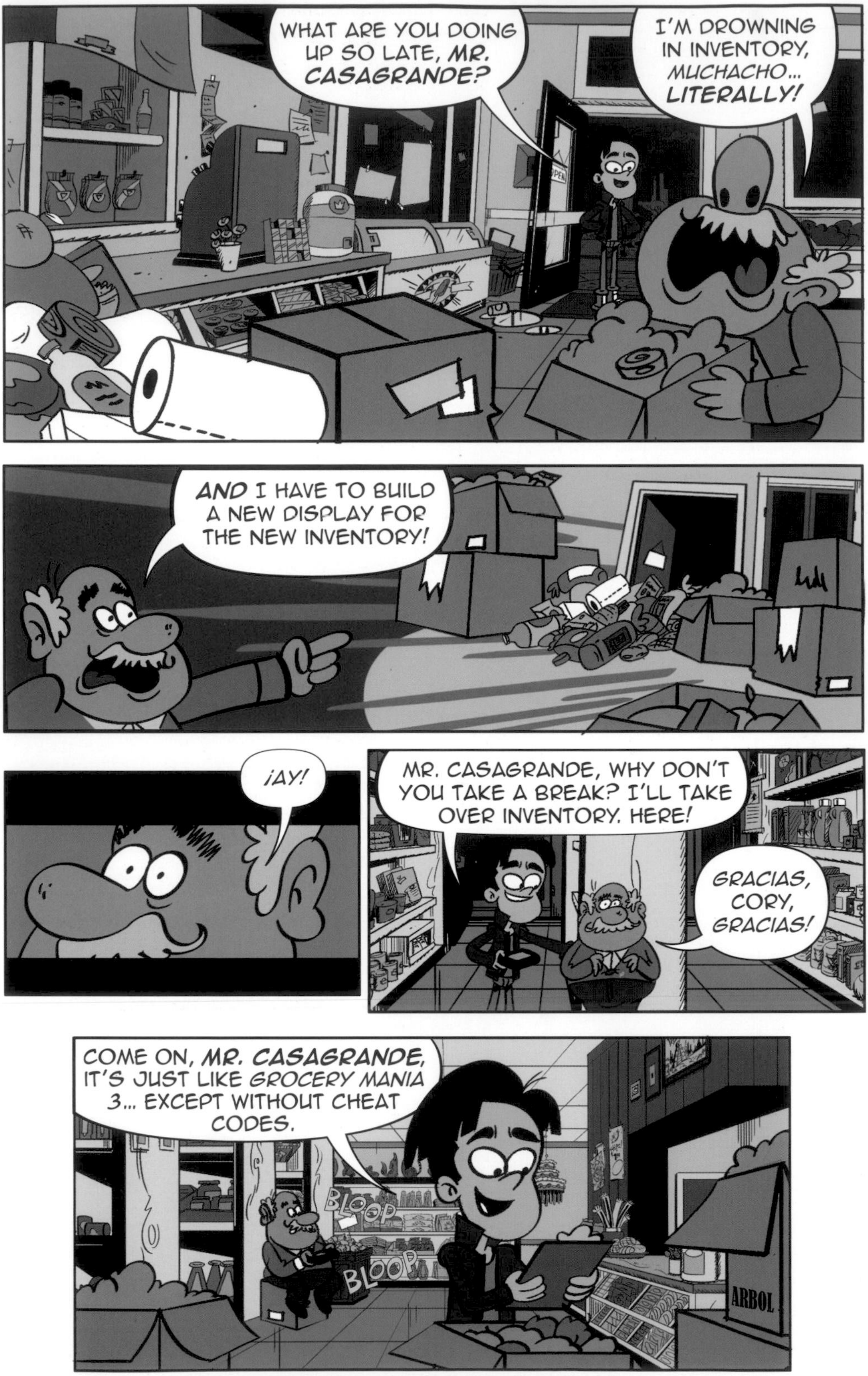
WHAT ARE YOU DOING UP SO LATE, MR. CASAGRANDE?
I'M DROWNING IN INVENTORY, MUCHACHO... LITERALLY!
OPEN
AND I HAVE TO BUILD A NEW DISPLAY FOR THE NEW INVENTORY!
¡AY!
MR. CASAGRANDE, WHY DON'T YOU TAKE A BREAK? I'LL TAKE OVER INVENTORY. HERE!
GRACIAS, CORY, GRACIAS!
COME ON, MR. CASAGRANDE, IT'S JUST LIKE GROCERY MANIA 3... EXCEPT WITHOUT CHEAT CODES.
BLOOP
BLOOP
ARBOL

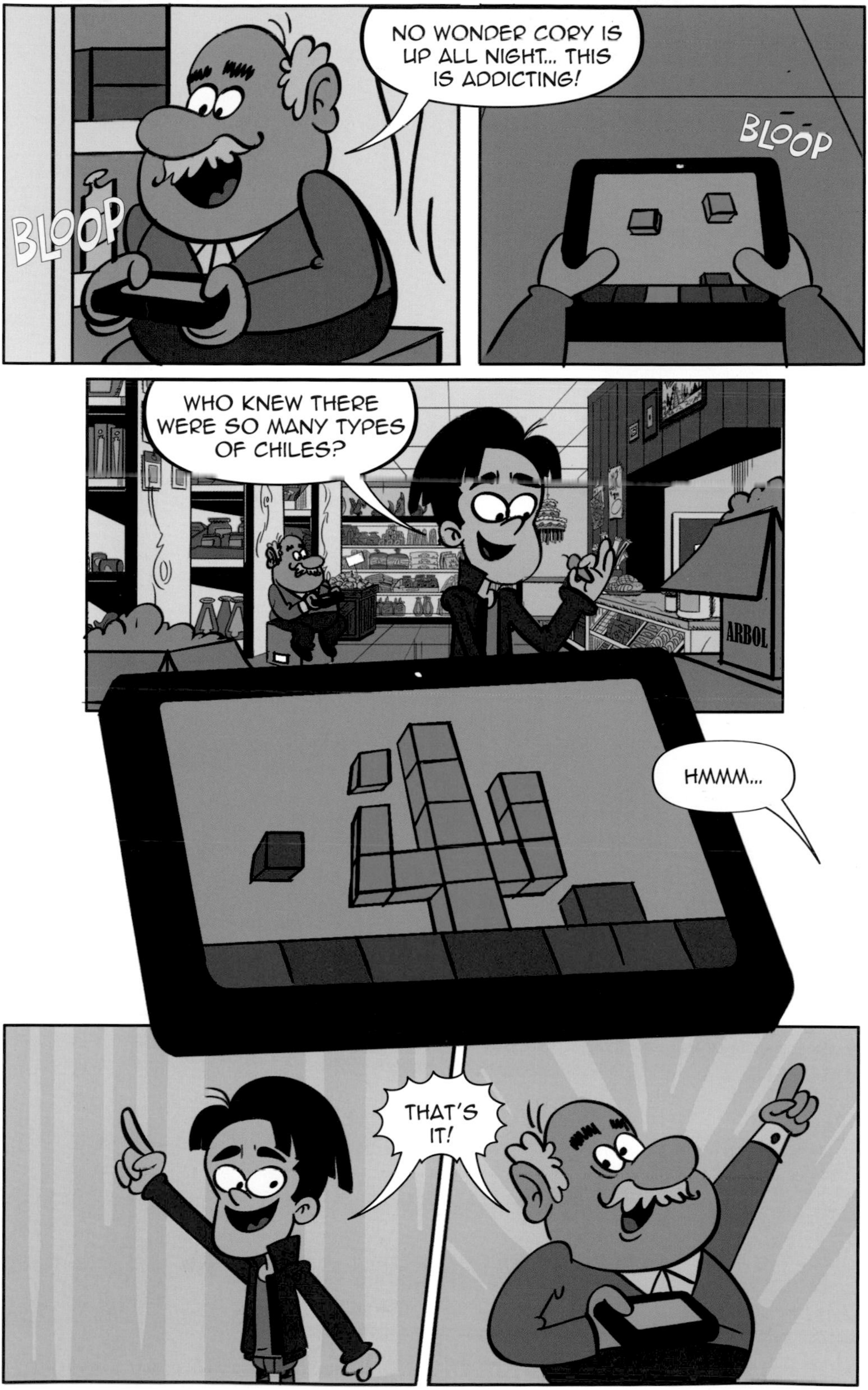
NO WONDER CORY IS UP ALL NIGHT... THIS IS ADDICTING!
BLOOP
BLOOP
WHO KNEW THERE WERE SO MANY TYPES OF CHILES?
ARBOL
HMMM...
THAT'S IT!

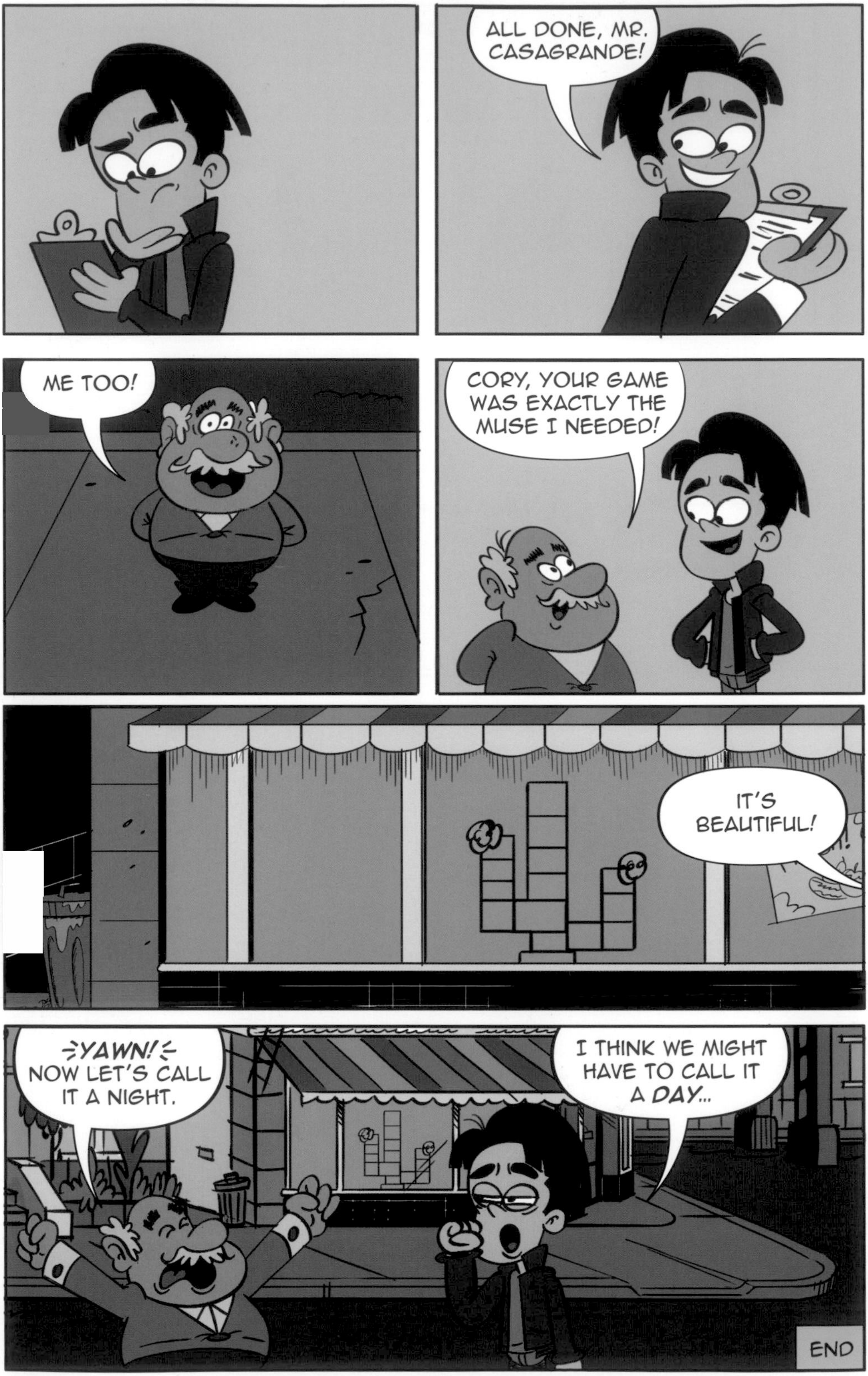
ALL DONE, MR. CASAGRANDE!
ME TOO!
CORY, YOUR GAME WAS EXACTLY THE MUSE I NEEDED!
IT'S BEAUTIFUL!
=YAWN!= NOW LET'S CALL IT A NIGHT.
I THINK WE MIGHT HAVE TO CALL IT A *DAY*...
END

"BACK TO THE BOOGIE"

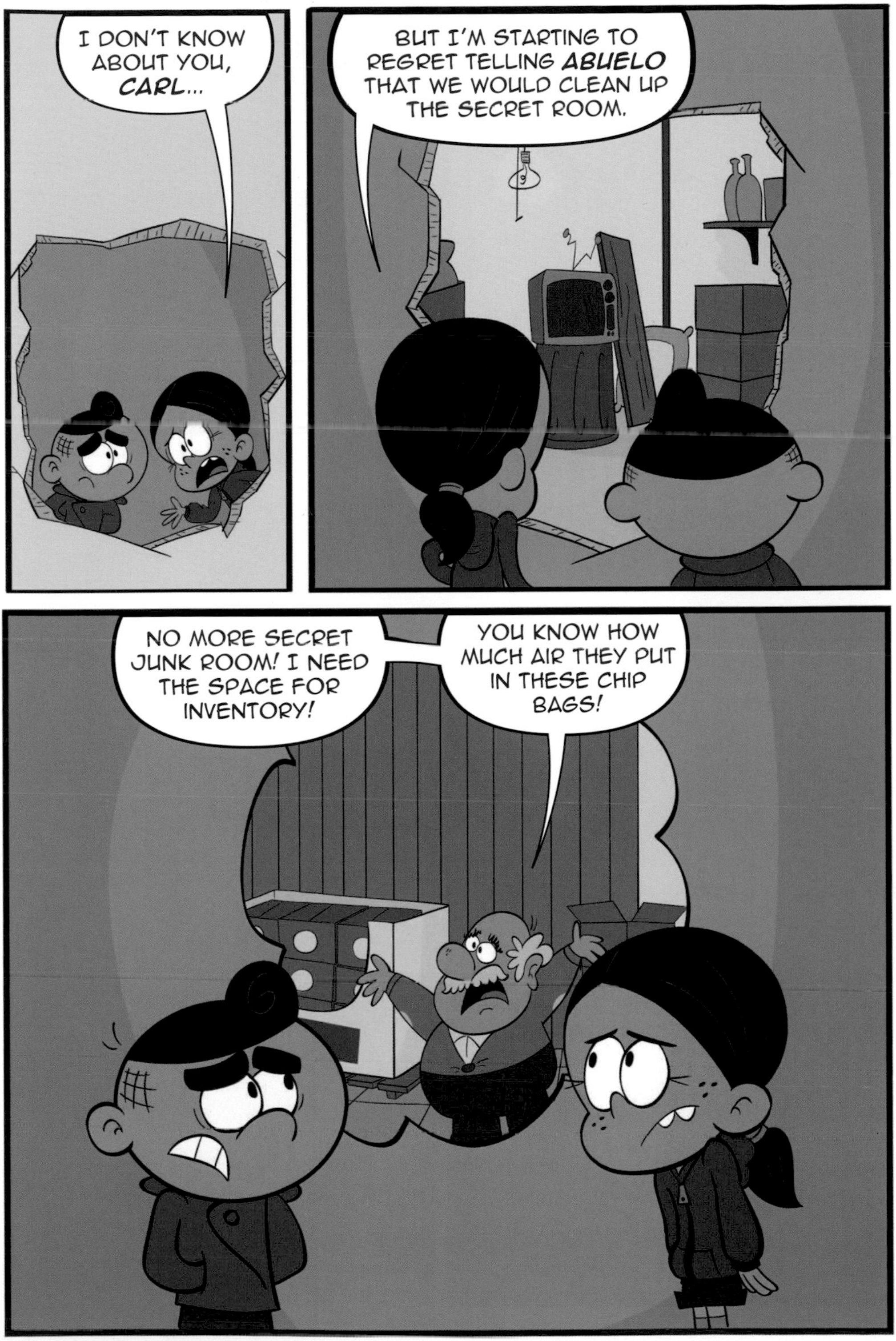
I DON'T KNOW ABOUT YOU, CARL...
BUT I'M STARTING TO REGRET TELLING ABUELO THAT WE WOULD CLEAN UP THE SECRET ROOM.
NO MORE SECRET JUNK ROOM! I NEED THE SPACE FOR INVENTORY!
YOU KNOW HOW MUCH AIR THEY PUT IN THESE CHIP BAGS!

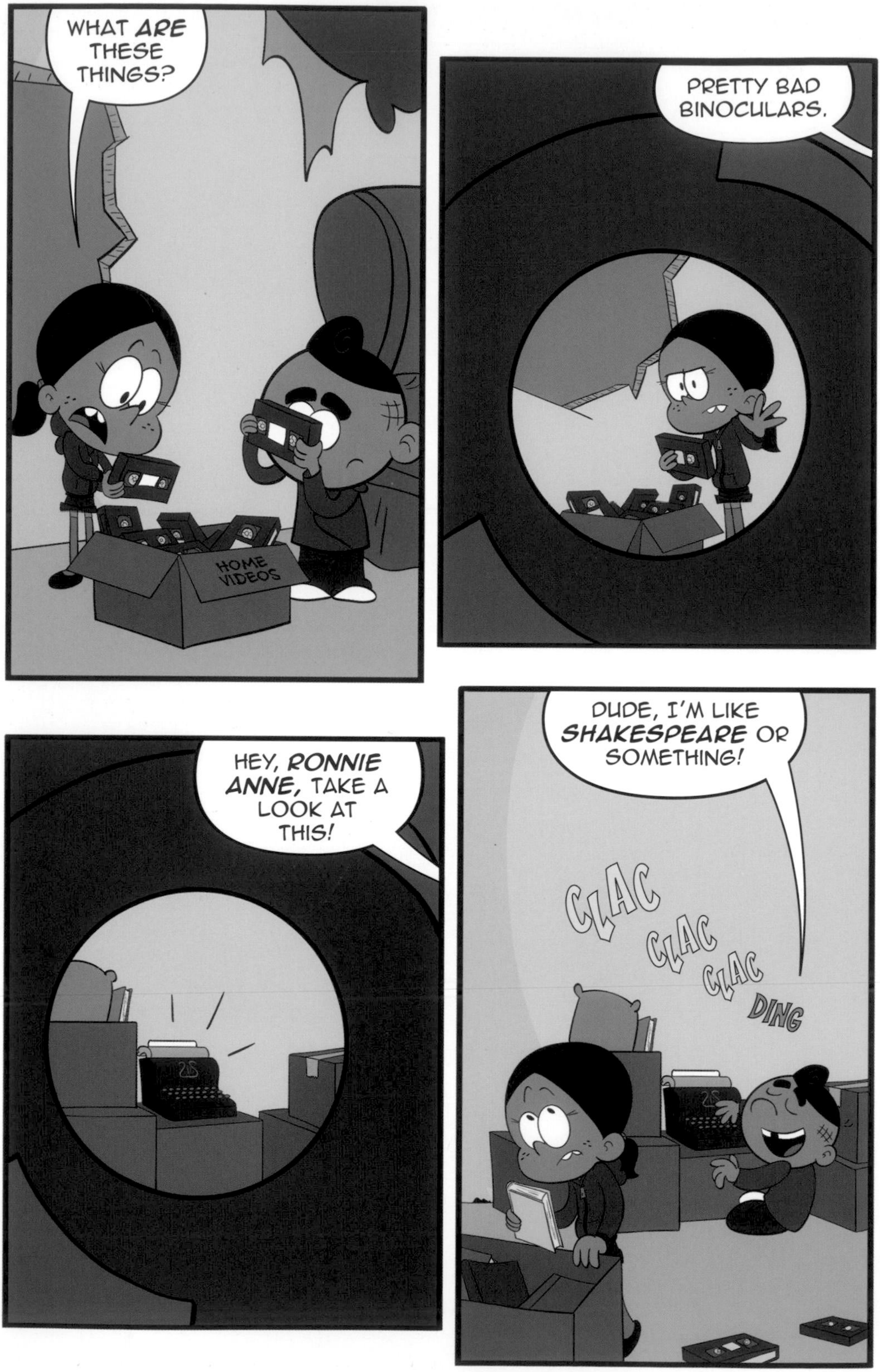
WHAT ARE THESE THINGS?
HOME VIDEOS
PRETTY BAD BINOCULARS.
HEY, RONNIE ANNE, TAKE A LOOK AT THIS!
DUDE, I'M LIKE SHAKESPEARE OR SOMETHING!
CLAC
CLAC
CLAC
DING

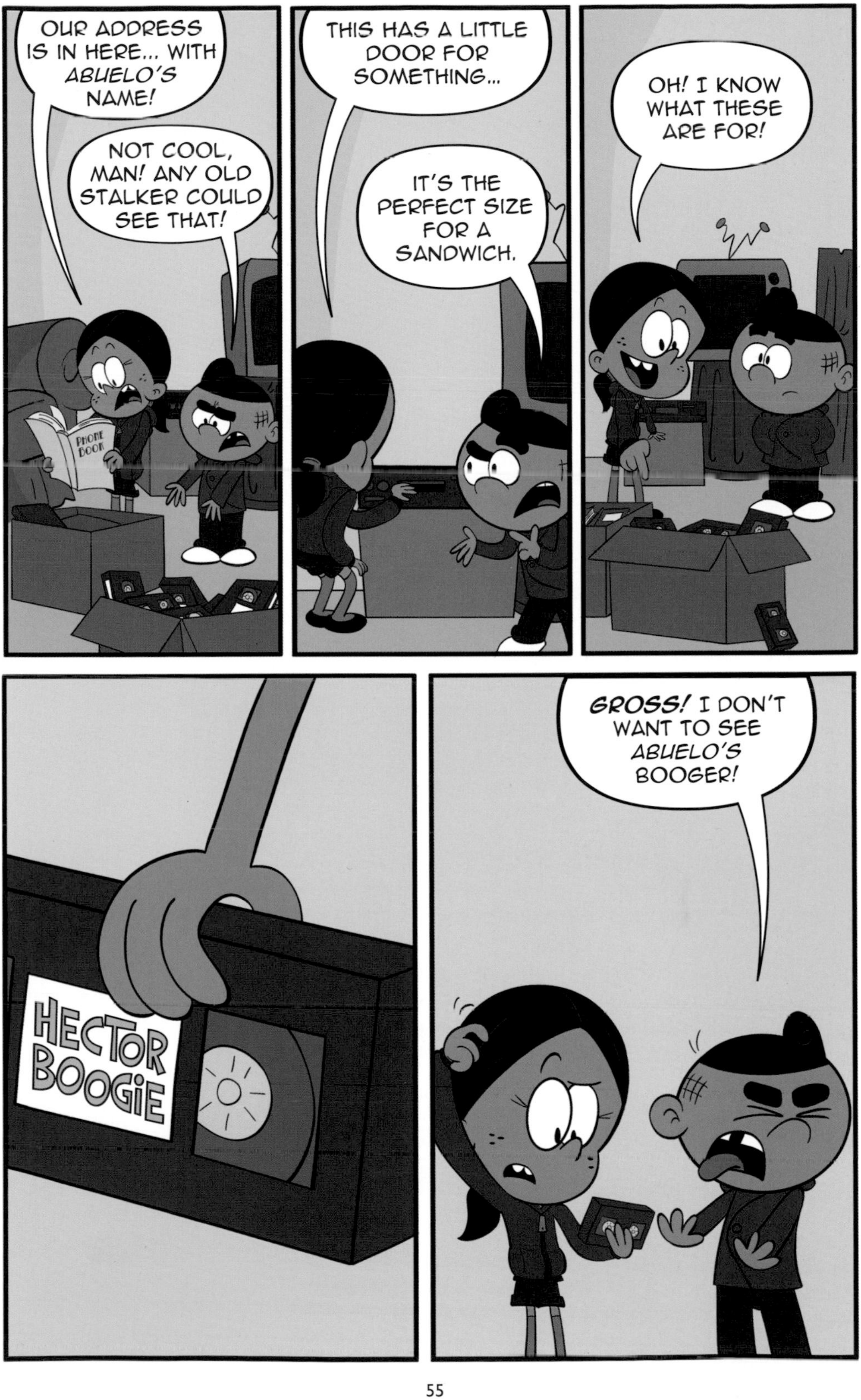
OUR ADDRESS IS IN HERE... WITH ABUELO'S NAME!
PHONE BOOK
NOT COOL, MAN! ANY OLD STALKER COULD SEE THAT!
THIS HAS A LITTLE DOOR FOR SOMETHING...
IT'S THE PERFECT SIZE FOR A SANDWICH.
OH! I KNOW WHAT THESE ARE FOR!
HECTOR BOOGIE
GROSS! I DON'T WANT TO SEE ABUELO'S BOOGER!

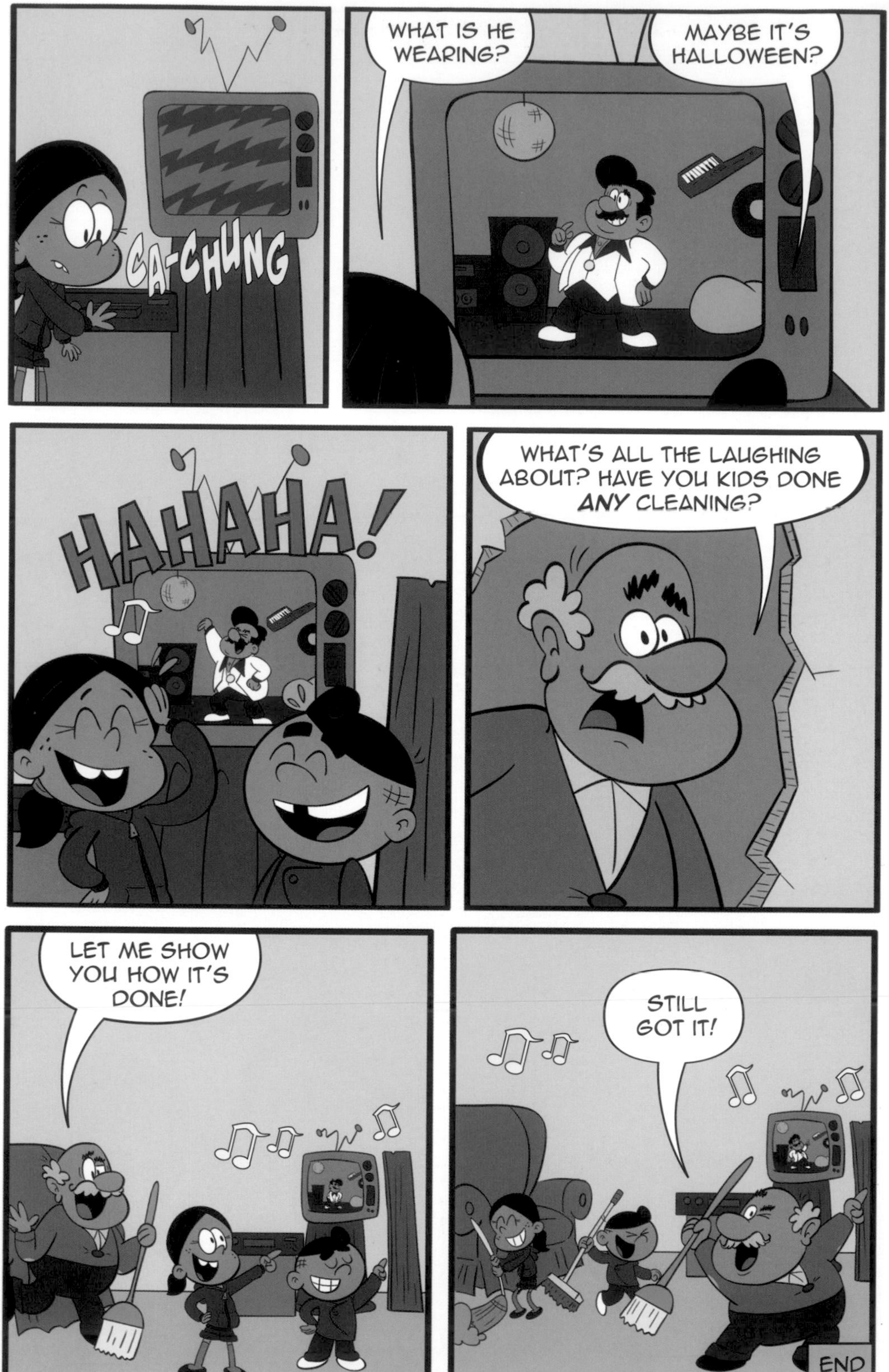

CA-CHUNG
WHAT IS HE WEARING?
MAYBE IT'S HALLOWEEN?
HAHAHA!
WHAT'S ALL THE LAUGHING ABOUT? HAVE YOU KIDS DONE ANY CLEANING?
LET ME SHOW YOU HOW IT'S DONE!
STILL GOT IT!
END

"SPAR WITH PAR"

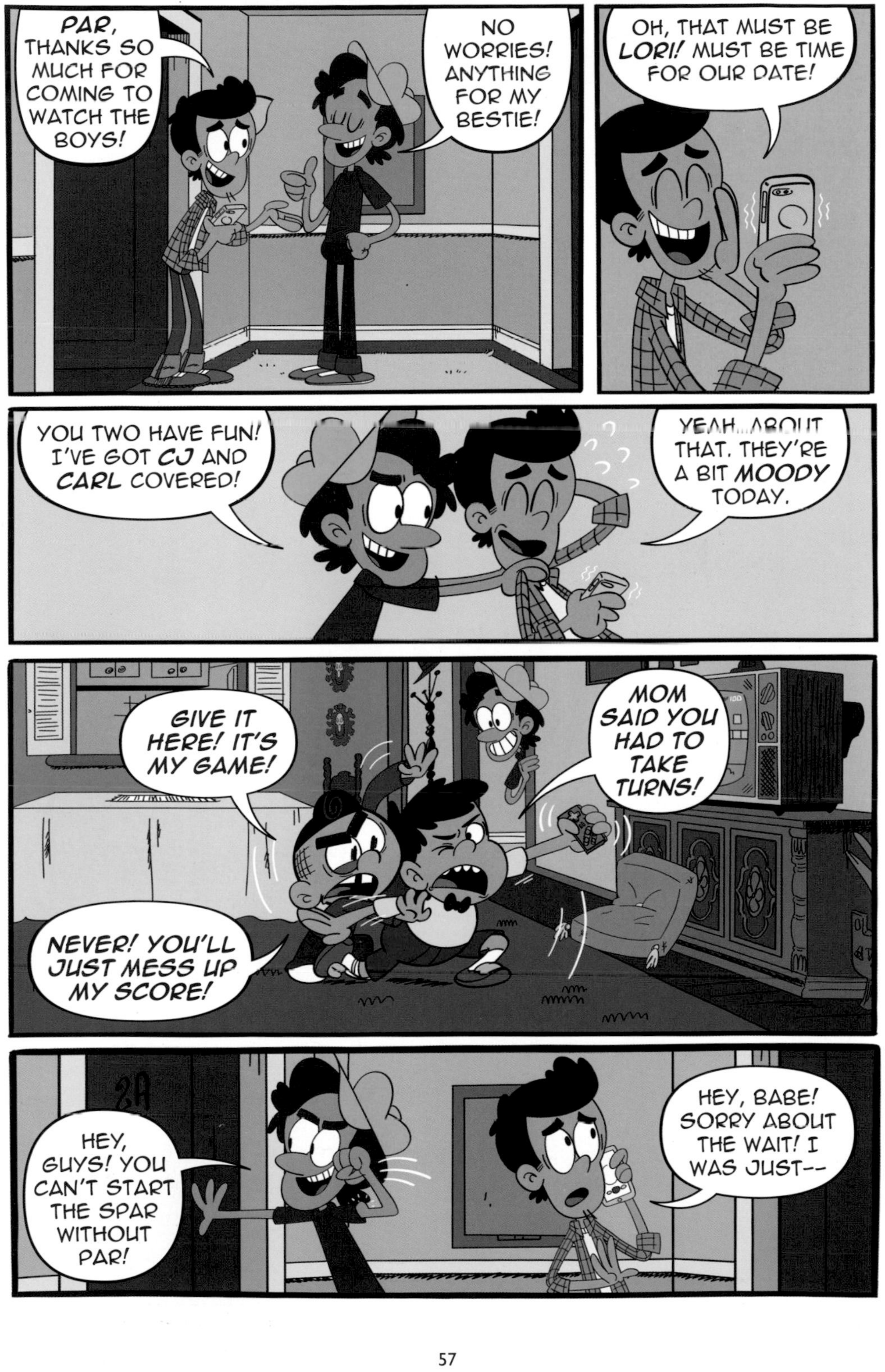

PAR, THANKS SO MUCH FOR COMING TO WATCH THE BOYS!
NO WORRIES! ANYTHING FOR MY BESTIE!
OH, THAT MUST BE LORI! MUST BE TIME FOR OUR DATE!
YOU TWO HAVE FUN! I'VE GOT CJ AND CARL COVERED!
YEAH...ABOUT THAT. THEY'RE A BIT MOODY TODAY.
GIVE IT HERE! IT'S MY GAME!
MOM SAID YOU HAD TO TAKE TURNS!
NEVER! YOU'LL JUST MESS UP MY SCORE!
HEY, GUYS! YOU CAN'T START THE SPAR WITHOUT PAR!
HEY, BABE! SORRY ABOUT THE WAIT! I WAS JUST--

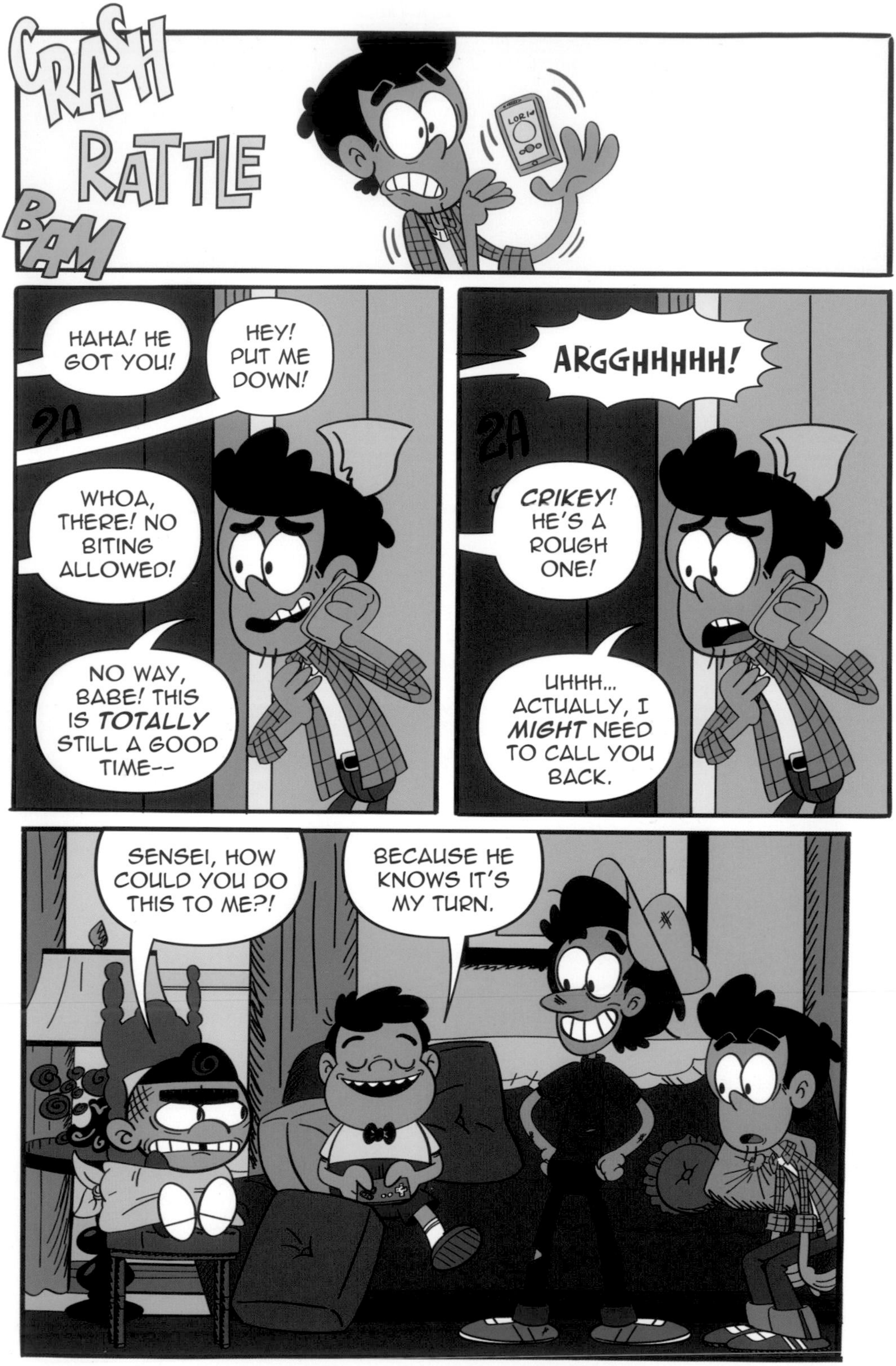
CRASH
RATTLE
BAM
LORI
HAHA! HE GOT YOU!
HEY! PUT ME DOWN!
2A
WHOA, THERE! NO BITING ALLOWED!
NO WAY, BABE! THIS IS TOTALLY STILL A GOOD TIME--
ARGGHHHHH!
2A
CRIKEY! HE'S A ROUGH ONE!
UHHH... ACTUALLY, I MIGHT NEED TO CALL YOU BACK.
SENSEI, HOW COULD YOU DO THIS TO ME?!
BECAUSE HE KNOWS IT'S MY TURN.

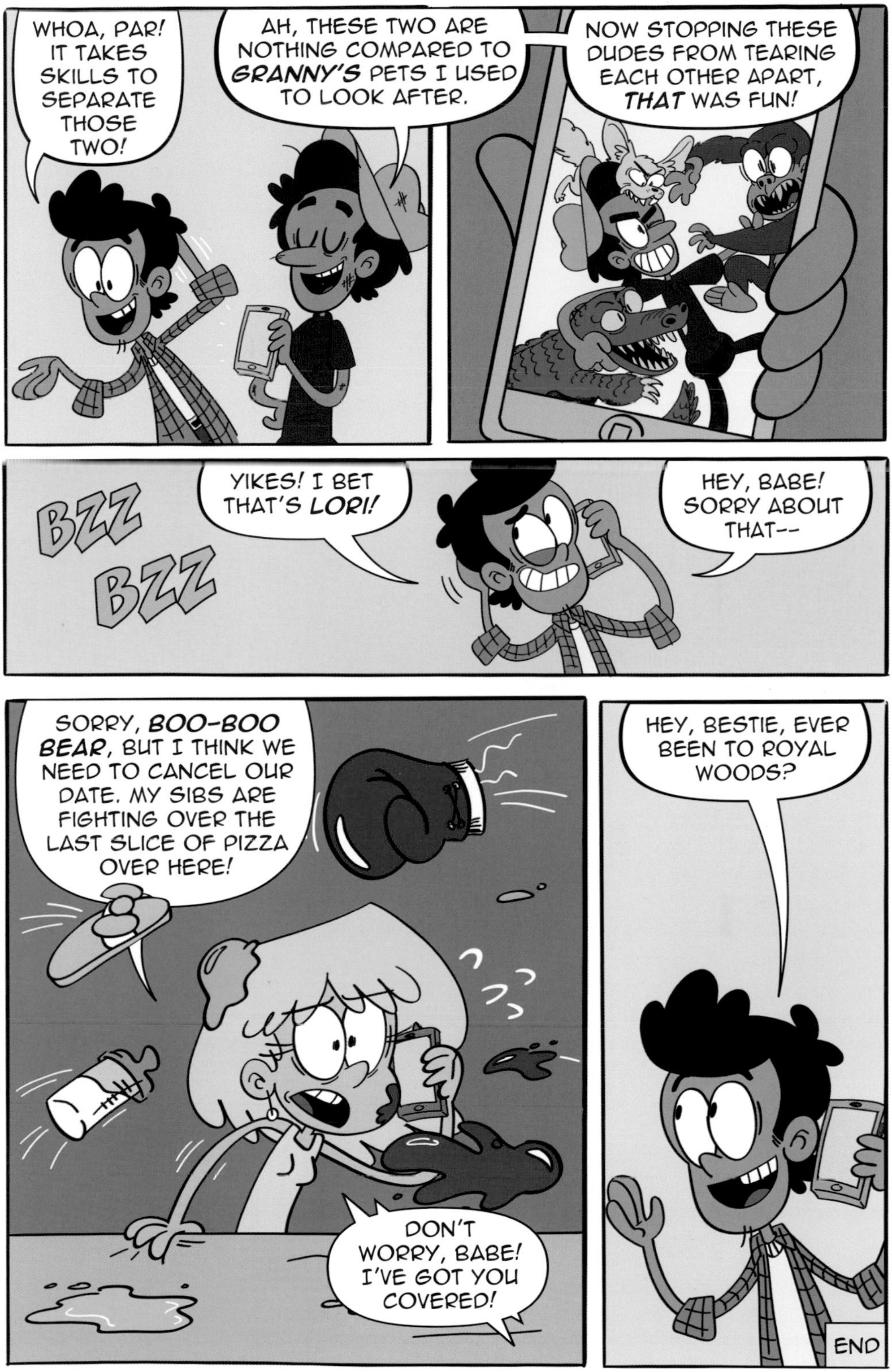
WHOA, PAR! IT TAKES SKILLS TO SEPARATE THOSE TWO!
AH, THESE TWO ARE NOTHING COMPARED TO **GRANNY'S** PETS I USED TO LOOK AFTER.
NOW STOPPING THESE DUDES FROM TEARING EACH OTHER APART, **THAT** WAS FUN!
BZZ BZZ
YIKES! I BET THAT'S **LORI!**
HEY, BABE! SORRY ABOUT THAT--
SORRY, **BOO-BOO BEAR**, BUT I THINK WE NEED TO CANCEL OUR DATE. MY SIBS ARE FIGHTING OVER THE LAST SLICE OF PIZZA OVER HERE!
DON'T WORRY, BABE! I'VE GOT YOU COVERED!
HEY, BESTIE, EVER BEEN TO ROYAL WOODS?
END

nickelodeon
NICKELODEON'S HIT NEW ANIMATED SHOW
THE LOUD HOUSE
THERE WILL BE CHAOS
PAPERCUTZ

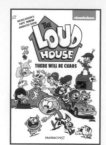

THE LOUD HOUSE
#1
"There Will Be Chaos"

nickelodeon
THE LOUD HOUSE
THERE WILL BE CHAOS

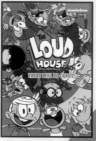

THE LOUD HOUSE
#2
"There Will Be More Chaos"

nickelodeon
NICKELODEON'S #1 HIT ANIMATED SHOW
THE LOUD HOUSE
LIVE LIFE LOUD!

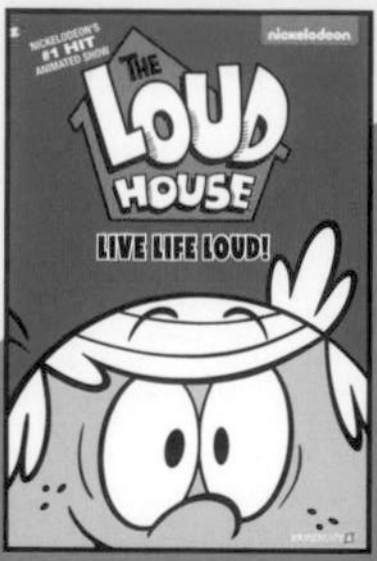

THE LOUD HOUSE
#3
"Live Life Loud!"

nickelodeon
THE LOUD HOUSE
FAMILY TREE
KEEP OUT!

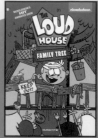

THE LOUD HOUSE
#4
"Family Tree"

nickelodeon
NICKELODEON'S HIT ANIMATED SHOW
THE LOUD HOUSE
AFTER DARK

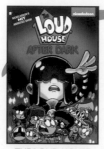

THE LOUD HOUSE
#5
"After Dark"

nickelodeon
NICKELODEON'S HIT SHOW
THE LOUD HOUSE
LOUD & PROUD
PAPERCUTZ

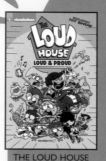

THE LOUD HOUSE
#6
"Loud & Proud"

nickelodeon
NICKELODEON'S HIT ANIMATED SHOW
THE LOUD HOUSE
THE STRUGGLE IS REAL

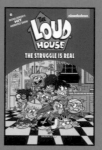

THE LOUD HOUSE
#7
"The Struggle is Real"

nickelodeon
THE LOUD HOUSE
Livin' La Casa Loud!
PAPERCUTZ

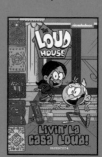

THE LOUD HOUSE
#8
"Livin' La Casa Loud!"

nickelodeon
FROM NICKELODEON'S HIT ANIMATED SHOW
THE LOUD HOUSE
ULTIMATE HANGOUT

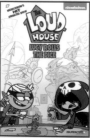

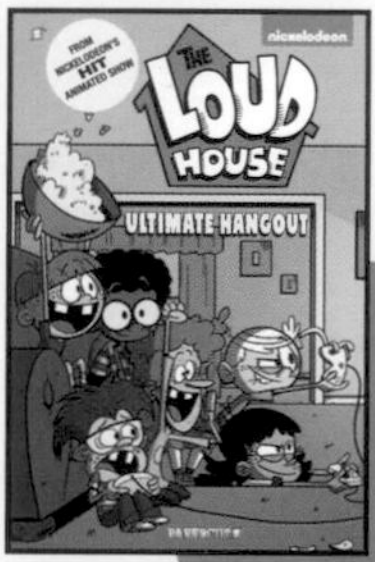

THE LOUD HOUSE
#9
"Ultimate Hangout"

nickelodeon
NICKELODEON'S EMMY-WINNING ANIMATED SHOW
THE LOUD HOUSE
THE MANY FACES OF LINCOLN LOUD
PAPERCUTZ

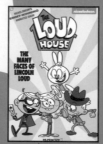

THE LOUD HOUSE
#10
"The Many Faces of
Lincoln Loud"

nickelodeon
THE LOUD HOUSE
WHO'S THE LOUDEST?
PAPERCUTZ

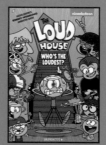

THE LOUD HOUSE
#11
"Who's the Loudest?"

nickelodeon
THE LOUD HOUSE
THE CASE OF THE STOLEN DRAWERS
PAPERCUTZ

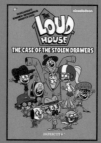

THE LOUD HOUSE
#12
"The Case of the Stolen
Drawers"

nickelodeon
NICKELODEON'S HIT ANIMATED SHOW
THE LOUD HOUSE
LUCY ROLLS THE DICE
PAPERCUTZ

THE LOUD HOUSE
#13
"Lucy Rolls the Dice"

nickelodeon
NICKELODEON'S HIT ANIMATED SHOW
THE LOUD HOUSE
GUESSING GAMES
PAPERCUTZ

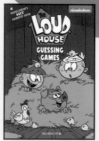

THE LOUD HOUSE
#14
"Guessing Games"

nickelodeon
THE LOUD HOUSE
THE MISSING LINC
PAPERCUTZ

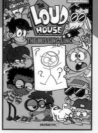

THE LOUD HOUSE
#15
"The Missing Linc"

nickelodeon
THE LOUD HOUSE
LOUD AND CLEAR

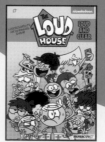

THE LOUD HOUSE
#16
"Loud and Clear"

COMING SOON

nickelodeon
NICKELODEON'S HIT ANIMATED SHOW
THE LOUD HOUSE
SIBLING RIVALRY
PAPERCUTZ

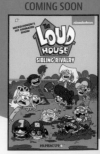

THE LOUD HOUSE
#17
"Sibling Rivalry"

THE LOUD HOUSE	THE LOUD HOUSE	THE LOUD HOUSE	THE LOUD HOUSE	THE LOUD HOUSE
3 IN 1	3 IN 1	3 IN 1	3 IN 1	3 IN 1
#1	#2	#3	#4	#5

COMING SOON

THE CASAGRANDES	THE CASAGRANDES	THE CASAGRANDES	THE CASAGRANDES
#1	#2	#3	3 IN 1
"We're All Familia"	"Anything for Familia"	"Brand Stinkin' New"	#1

THE LOUD HOUSE	THE LOUD HOUSE	THE LOUD HOUSE	THE LOUD HOUSE
WINTER SPECIAL	SUMMER SPECIAL	LOVE OUT LOUD SPECIAL	BACK TO SCHOOL SPECIAL

THE LOUD HOUSE and THE CASAGRANDES graphic novels and specials are available for $7.99 each in paperback, $12.99 each in hardcover. THE LOUD HOUSE 3 IN 1 and THE CASAGRANDES 3 IN 1 graphic novels are available for $14.99 each in paperback only.

Available from booksellers everywhere. You can also order online from Papercutz.com, or call 1-800-886-1223, Monday through Friday, 9-5 EST. MC, Visa, and AmEx accepted. To order by mail, please add $5.00 for postage and handling for the first book ordered, $1.00 for each additional book and make check payable to NBM Publishing. Send to: Papercutz, 160 Broadway, Suite 700, East Wing, New York, NY 10038.

The Loud House and The Casagrandes graphic novels are also available digitally wherever e-books are sold.

WATCH OUT FOR PAPERCUTZ™

¡Hola! Welcome to the family-phone-plan-free THE CASAGRANDES #4 "Friends and Family," from Papercutz, those social-networking netizens dedicated to publishing great graphic novels for all ages. I'm Jim Salicrup, the Editor-in-Chief and Frequent *Mercado* Shopper, here to let you know that there are all sorts of other Papercutz graphic novels featuring either the Casagrande's family or their friends from THE LOUD HOUSE coming soon…

NICKELODEON'S HIT ANIMATED SHOW
nickelodeon
THE LOUD HOUSE
SIBLING RIVALRY
PAPERCUTZ

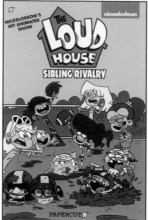

First up, is a book that's perfect for those fans of THE CASAGRANDES who are just joining us, and perhaps fretting that you've missed out on the fun to be found in THE CASAGRANDES first three graphic novels. The good news is that THE CASAGRANDES 3 IN 1 #1 is coming! As the title implies, this book is a collection of that trio of graphic novels. This book features all the comics, all the characters, and all the fun that was included in the first three THE CASAGRANDES graphic novels. Of course, if you've already got those graphic novels, you may consider this collected edition an ideal gift for someone you know who also enjoys THE CASAGRANDES. You know, like a friend or family member?

Second, is THE LOUD HOUSE #17 "Sibling Rivalry," the latest volume in the Nickelodeon graphic novel series that started it all. What do I mean? Well, as all faithful fans of THE CASAGRANDES know, Ronnie Anne and Bobbie Santiago first appeared on THE LOUD HOUSE animated TV series. Likewise, when THE LOUD HOUSE became a Papercutz graphic novel series, Ronnie Anne and Bobbie were included too! So, THE LOUD HOUSE series holds a special spot in the hearts of all fans of THE CASAGRANDES. The good news is THE LOUD HOUSE TV show and the graphic novels are both big hits and are more fun than ever! Of course, Lincoln Loud is still having fun and conflicts with his ten sisters, not to mention his ever-expanding group of friends. And as fans of the graphic novels know, you'll often find stories starring characters that often don't get to be in the spotlight on the TV series. To get an even better idea of what awaits you THE LOUD HOUSE #17 "Sibling Rivalry," just check out the special sneak preview on the next page.

Third, is a special edition of THE LOUD HOUSE called "Super Special," which is focused on the super-heroic and fantastic characters that both Lincoln Loud and his best bud Clyde McBride, not to mention Ronnie Anne Santiago, admire. From Ace Savvy to Muscle Fish, see why these larger-than-life characters have earned Lincoln and Clyde's adoration, compelling them to collect their comics, play their video games and covet their action figures. I suspect that Carl Casagrande and his favorite superhero, El Falcon de Fuego, will probably pop up in this super-spectacular "Super Special."

Fourth and finally, it should be pointed out that all these graphic novels, plus all the previous volumes of THE LOUD HOUSE, are not only available at booksellers everywhere, online, bookstores, comics shops, one mercado, and book fairs, but also at libraries, where you can enjoy these comical comics for free. They're also all available digitally wherever e-books are sold.

And if all those graphic novels starring THE CASAGRANDES, THE LOUD HOUSE, and their friends and families, weren't enough to satisfy your graphic novel needs, don't forget that Papercutz publishes plenty of other graphic novels that you may enjoy—everything from THE SMURFS, who also appear on Nickelodeon and in several graphic novel series, to such fun series as THE QUEEN'S FAVORITE WITCH, GILLBERT, THE NIGHTMARE BRIGADE, and many more. Just browse our site at papercutz.com and subscribe to our free e-newsletter and we're sure you'll find something you'll love!

Hey, allow me to make a little confession. At the end of the last paragraph, it wasn't easy picking just three additional Papercutz graphic novels to mention. I could've just as easily mentioned the world-wide best-selling ASTERIX series, or THE FLY, or DANCE CLASS, or any of our other Papercutz titles. It was like trying to pick your favorite friends and family—it's hard because you love them all! So, friends, let it be known that we consider you a part of the Papercutz family, and we hope to see you again in the fifth graphic novel of THE CASAGRANDES!

Gracias,

Jim

STAY IN TOUCH!

EMAIL:	salicrup@papercutz.com
WEB:	papercutz.com
TWITTER:	@papercutzgn
INSTAGRAM:	@papercutzgn
FACEBOOK:	PAPERCUTZGRAPHICNOVELS
FANMAIL:	Papercutz, 160 Broadway, Suite 700, East Wing, New York, NY 10038

Go to papercutz.com and sign up for the free Papercutz e-newsletter!

Exclusive preview of THE LOUD HOUSE #17 "Sibling Rivalry"

"TRENDFRETTER"

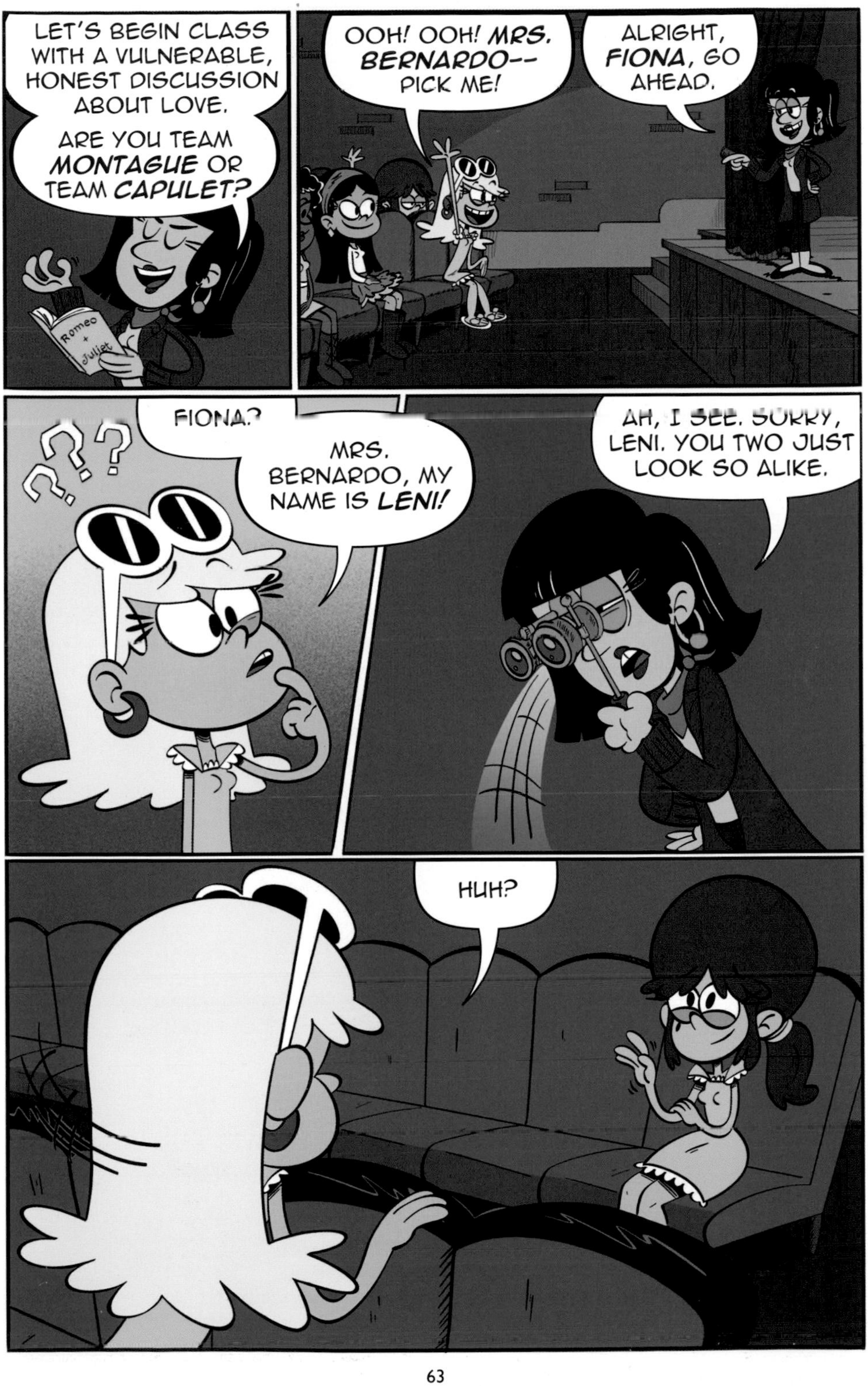
LET'S BEGIN CLASS WITH A VULNERABLE, HONEST DISCUSSION ABOUT LOVE.
ARE YOU TEAM MONTAGUE OR TEAM CAPULET?
Romeo + Juliet
OOH! OOH! MRS. BERNARDO-- PICK ME!
ALRIGHT, FIONA, GO AHEAD.
FIONA?
MRS. BERNARDO, MY NAME IS LENI!
AH, I SEE. SORRY, LENI. YOU TWO JUST LOOK SO ALIKE.
HUH?

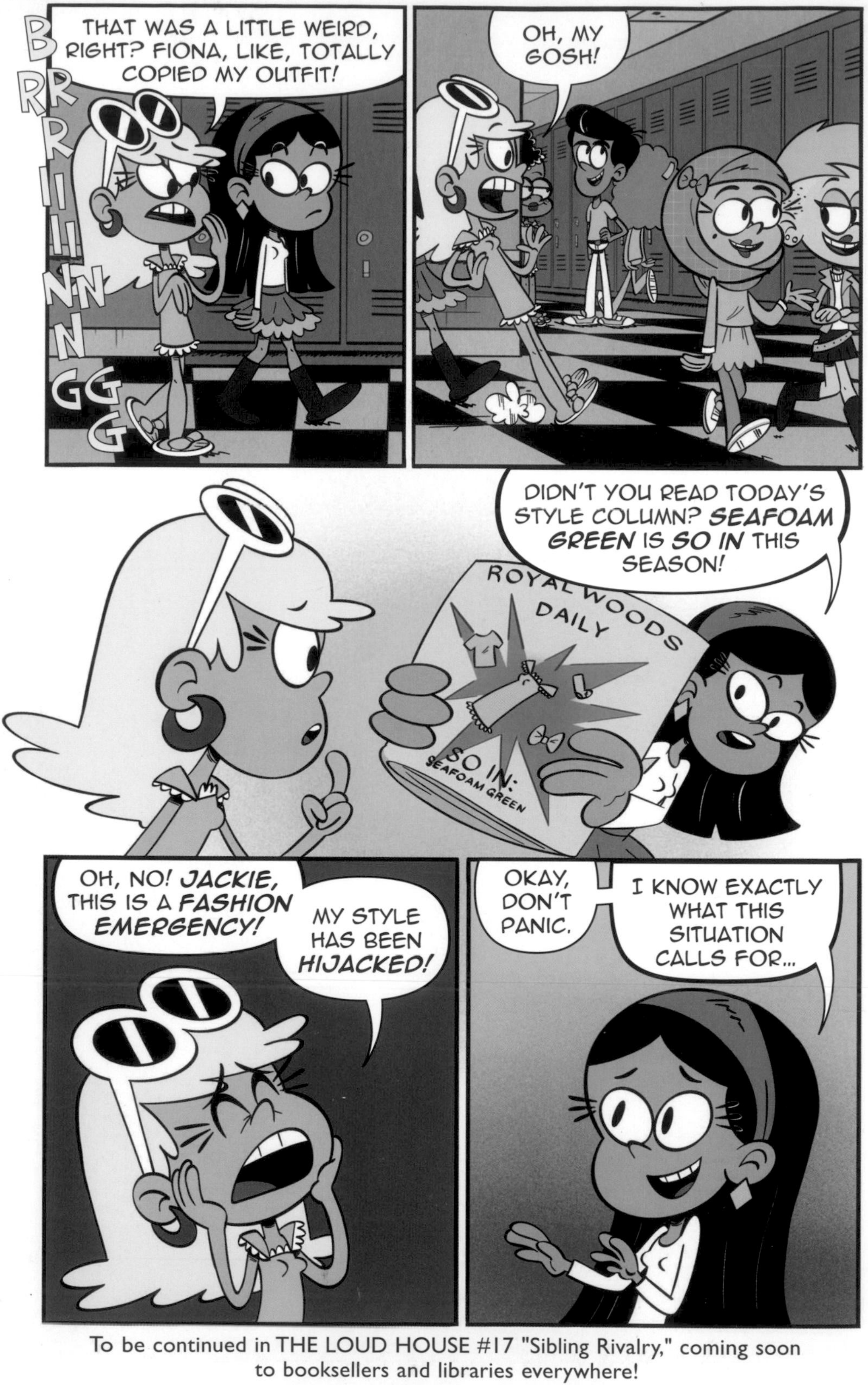
BRRRIIIINNNNGGG
THAT WAS A LITTLE WEIRD, RIGHT? FIONA, LIKE, TOTALLY COPIED MY OUTFIT!
OH, MY GOSH!
DIDN'T YOU READ TODAY'S STYLE COLUMN? SEAFOAM GREEN IS SO IN THIS SEASON!
ROYAL WOODS DAILY
SO IN: SEAFOAM GREEN
OH, NO! JACKIE, THIS IS A FASHION EMERGENCY!
MY STYLE HAS BEEN HIJACKED!
OKAY, DON'T PANIC.
I KNOW EXACTLY WHAT THIS SITUATION CALLS FOR...

To be continued in THE LOUD HOUSE #17 "Sibling Rivalry," coming soon to booksellers and libraries everywhere!